Dear Carol,

I hope you
book. It's so great
meet a fellow author +
lawyer!

♡ Mlnia

All Honest Pilgrims

ACKNOWLEDGMENTS

Lucia Nelson Publishing, LLC
607 E Boston Post Road
Mamaroneck, NY 10543
www.lucianelsonpublishing.com

Cover photo of Walden Pond Maria Valente
Author photo Elyse Carter

ISBN: 979 8 6916 9444 8

First Addition

DEDICATION

This book is dedicated to:

Alana and Michael who are the driving force behind everything I do.
The best kids any mother could hope for.
Joe, Tommy, Gabby, Valentina and "?." You are my hope for the
future, and you are my inspiration. I do this all for you.
Samantha and Gerard your love for my children and grandchildren
brings me such peace and happiness.
Corinne, Christine, Joe, Debby and Sal who walked me through this
process and whose wisdom, encouragement and help allowed me to
finally get this out there after it resided in my head and on my hard
drive for 20 years.
To Jean, Donna, Roxanne and Michele who exemplify everything I
can only hope to be.
To Mr. Leonard who first put a copy of <u>Walden</u> in my hand and
started this whole pilgrimage for me.
To all my guardian angels especially, Grandma whose example of a
strong independent woman inspires me daily, and Mom and Dad,
members of the Greatest Generation. It was a privilege to have you
as parents, and an honor to care for you in your final years. I love
and miss you daily. I hope I make you proud.
And…To HDT whose genius inspired me and so many others.
Finally, to all the 'pilgrims' who read this and find solace and hope in
these pages. I wrote this for you.

"I should not talk so much about myself if there were anybody else whom I knew as well."

Henry David Thoreau.

For this reason, each chapter is told by the character in first person.

Billy Chapter 1

"We slander the hyena; man is the fiercest and cruelest animal." Henry David
Thoreau

When I was a kid, I was overweight. I was constantly picked on and
teased for having the audacity to be both smart and fat. I rode the big
yellow bus to grammar school. Forty-five torturous minutes each way,
every day. My parents were American born, but old school Italian who
worked wicked hard and ran a successful butcher shop in the North End
of Boston. They didn't understand a fat boy's need to dress like all the
other kids to try to fit in. I took a lot of teasing because of my clothes. I
would dread going to school because it was always the same thing. I
would walk to the bus stop and Ted Harmon would be waiting for me.
He was this obnoxious farm boy from upstate New York who was living
with his aunt and uncle for a year. I was in fourth grade and he was in
fifth. As soon as I got there, he would have his hand out and I would
have to relinquish my milk money. The first few times he asked me for it,
I refused. He responded by ripping the arm off my jacket one day and
the pocket off my pants the next. My mother got mad because we could
not afford to have perfectly good clothes turned into rags. She told me to
just give him what he wants; it would be cheaper in the long run. It never
occurred to her to call Ted's aunt or even to drive me to school to put me
out of my misery. It was just one of those things she thought I had to get
through. More likely, she was just too busy to think about it at all.

After the humiliation of having my milk money extorted every morning, I
would get on the bus and for the next forty-five minutes be spit on, hit,
slapped, kicked, mimicked, and teased because I was fat. It was relentless.
The bus driver just kept driving and never tried to stop them. I tried to
fight back the tears, but often just sat there and silently felt them rolling
down my face and there was nothing I could do to stop them. Inside I
was screaming silently. If I lifted my hand to wipe my eyes, one of the

bullies would notice. If one of them caught sight of me crying, the whole bus would break into a mock chorus of tears.

It went on like this until the day when I finally had enough. Ted was being particularly brutal that day. He did his usual extortion routine at the bus stop, then got on the bus and decided that he was going to sit in the seat with me so he could torture me up close. I knew the moment he slithered into the seat next to me that this day was going to be one I would not soon forget. Sometimes you get those feelings. He started shoving me into the window, each time harder until my right arm began to ache from the constant crash against the hard metal. Then he pressed my stomach in like the Pillsbury dough boy. I couldn't take it anymore. I had endured enough of his torture, and today was the day it would end. I pushed as fast and hard as I could against him, and the bus must have been turning just the right way, because he fell off the seat and onto the filthy, slushy bus floor landing right on his sorry butt. The whole bus exploded in laughter, but the laughter ceased immediately when Ted got up and went for my throat. I could hear the other kids on the bus chanting for Ted, "kill him, kill him," as I felt his hands enclosing around my throat and felt blood rush to my neck. I thought they might get their way. He had me pinned in the seat and I couldn't get out. The idiot bus driver just kept driving, either oblivious to the fact that there was about to be a murder on his bus, or so unfeeling he really didn't care.

To this day, I do not know where I got the strength from, but I was able to get my hands up high enough to grab his hands. My chubby fingers encircled his wrists, and I dug my nails as deep into his flesh as I could. Then suddenly all the rage and anger that had built up inside me came out. I pried his hands off my neck, threw him to the ground and started to pound him. The kids on the bus were still chanting, but now they were chanting for me! They wanted to see me beat the crap out of Ted and there was nothing I wanted to do more than that. I got my first understanding of mob mentality that day. I kept hitting him and hitting him in the face with all the strength I could muster. He eventually got a bloody nose and the sight of his blood told me I better stop. I got off him, and still shaking crawled back into my seat just as the bus was pulling into the school parking lot. One of the kids in the front told the bus driver that Ted was bleeding, and he was unconscious. Everybody on the bus thought he was dead and for the first time ever there was silence.

The bus driver made one of the girls run inside to get the school nurse. He made his way towards Ted passing the rows of crying girls and silent boys. When he reached Ted he started to call his name, but there was no response. He was shaking him slightly and finally Ted stirred and started to come out of it. I watched all this from my bus seat with a combination of disbelief that I did this to someone, and a little glee that someone was Ted. There was also a tinge of guilt, but guilt was not my strongest emotion right now. Exhilaration was more the feeling of the moment. I got my first taste of blood, and I liked it. I felt like I had slayed the dragon that had been breathing the fires of hell down the back of my neck this past year.

I wanted to have this feeling for the rest of my life. I knew I hadn't killed Ted; he was too mean and nasty to die. But I had taught him a lesson that I hoped he would keep with him for a while. And maybe he would stop terrorizing people like me. If nothing else I earned back the right to keep my milk money and the bus was nevermore a war zone.

Chris Chapter 2

I'm a man who makes my living with words as a singer and songwriter in Nashville. It's a tough job. You don't dabble in it; you have to put your whole heart and soul in it. I do just that. It took a while for me to realize it was about more than making a barnload of money. There's a Thoreau quote that goes,

"Do not hire a man who does your work for money, but him who does it for love of it."

If you don't love what you're doing, it's going to show, and you won't never be able to make a go of it. It's kind of funny that my first hit, and maybe biggest came when I was still in college, back when I did everything for love, and not for money. I was born and bred in West Texas where I lived a pretty normal life. Daddy and Momma were both schoolteachers. We lived in Lubbock, which is probably the flattest place on the planet. There are no hills, not even any bumps in the road, just flat land as far as the eye could see. We get these dust storms blowing through every now and then. But that's about it for excitement. It's so open there you get the feeling like your living in a fishbowl. There's no place to hide. You're playing your life on a stage and all your neighbors are watching.

Because there's no privacy, people don't tend to rock the boat too much in Lubbock. Nobody wants to be the town scandal. I was no different. Growing up I was a good kid, a good student, involved in the community, church every Sunday and a good athlete…football was my thing. I stayed away from trouble and trouble didn't seem very interested in finding me either. My love was the guitar. I learned a few chords and picked up the rest mostly on my own. I wasn't very good, but man I loved to play that thing. I would go out to the garage because my Momma couldn't stand the racket I was making. I would try to sing like Garth Brooks, but I sounded more like a babbling brook. Heavy on the babble. The songs I made up were mostly sappy-high-school-hormone-driven love songs. It wasn't great music, but the process amazed me. Something I had as a thought in my head could come out through the guitar. My buddies Clay and Ronnie played the drums and fiddle as badly as I played the guitar. We decided to start a band and called ourselves the Lubbock Desperados. We figured Lubbock had a good music history as the home of the late Buddy Holly among others, so maybe something in the swirling, dusty air would eventually grab hold of us, and turn us into fine musical talent. That didn't seem to be happening any time soon.

I'm a big guy standing about 6'3 in boots and weigh in at 220lbs. Put me in a football uniform with full pads and I am intimidating. Texas Tech gave me a football scholarship. I was a lineman and damn good at it. My life spun around Friday nights. I loved being on the team and was serious about it too. I gave my coach 110% but didn't put as much effort into my schoolwork. I was passing everything, so I didn't feel the need to try much harder than that. Besides, football was only one semester long, I would buckle down during the winter.

I played my freshman year, then blew out my knee in a game against Nebraska. It was an illegal chop block. Man, did I hate the guy who did it to me. Now, looking back, I think he was like some kind of angel or something sent to change my life around. Sometimes you can be pointed in the right direction; other times you need a chop block to the knee to put you on the right path. I guess you get what you need even though you don't always know it at the time. Gifts are funny that way. Anyway, I needed surgery and was in a cast for the rest of the school year. During that time, I started to read a lot, and not just my assigned reading.

My Momma was an English teacher and a few years back had given me a copy of <u>Walden</u> by this guy *Henry David Thoreau.* It was one of those things you pack when you go away to college thinking you'll eventually get to it, but you're so busy goofing off and partying you never do. Well, now here it was, midway through the semester, my coursework was on cruise control, and I was laid up with this busted knee. The hours I spent working out and practicing were now empty. I picked up that copy of Walden and started reading it. The description of the flat, calmness of the Pond reminded me of the flat calmness of home, Lubbock. I read more. Soon I was attacking any book I could find by my man Henry. I declared English Literature as my major and took as many classes in American Lit as I could. If I hadn't been out of football, I never would have discovered how much enjoyment I could get out of reading.

As well as reading, I also started writing. First poetry...really bad poetry. Then I set my poetry to music and the second phase of my song-writing career had begun. My first few attempts were pathetic, but Clay and Ronnie stuck with me and went along with my sappy lyrics, and overly melancholy music. They were loyal Desperados. I always hoped one day I could repay them for being there for me during the early days.

I was enrolled in a creative writing class with this Professor, David Henry. He soon became my least favorite teacher. He was a real smart guy and had written a few books. He actually went on to become a pretty famous author, but he was trying to make me think too hard, and my head hurt every time I left that class. I was failing his class miserably. He would ask for a story featuring a fabulous reality. Now what the hell is that? He explained it as a sight or sound or something that happens unexpectedly and surprises you with its beauty or irony or humor.

He was very into light. Everything we studied involved light. There was Hemingway's clean well-lighted place for example, which I sort of got. Having been a budding musician, most of my free time was spent in dirty, poorly lit bars. A clean well-lighted place did sound a bit like heaven.

Anyway, I wrote this fabulous reality about a bullfighter that after he wins gets hit in the eye with a rose that is tossed to him from a fan and has to go to the hospital. Needless to say, I started the course with one foot in the hole. It's hard to climb back from a 'D', but somehow, eventually something clicked. I started to understand about the clean, well-lit places and fabulous realities and appreciate the authors he was making us read. I started to see Hemingway as a genius with a tortured soul instead of the spoiled brat I wanted to originally perceive him as. We started reading Thoreau and that's when everything came together for me.

My subsequent writing picked up more depth and color and I saw my grades climb from that first miserable 'D' to all 'A's. This class helped my musical career tremendously. Instead of the sappy garbage I had been writing, my songs were taking on a more mature, more meaningful turn to them. I was seeing each song as a work of art instead of just a piece to play and fill up three minutes. I became obsessed with writing and I needed to work on each song just as an artist would work on a painting until each stroke of the brush could combine perfectly to resemble something awesome. Each phrase was carefully crafted to convey the most meaning and imagery in the smallest amount of words. Clay and Ronnie saw the change in me and just went with the flow. They improved as I did, and we were really starting to sound like something.

My poetry, as I liked to call it, was becoming very popular among the college crowd me and the Desperados played to at Gary's. We had a standing gig every Saturday night at this local bar. It was cool to have people come up to us Monday morning in Psych class and tell us how much they loved our music. That's what we musicians live for.

Gary's was just a hop skip and a jump from campus, so the crowd was almost 100% Texas Tech. There was the occasional old man who wanders in for a Rheingold thinking it's 1945. Or a table of three or four middle-aged housewives who thought that by hanging out with kids their kid's age, they would gain some common ground with their own offspring and possibly have a conversation with them. This rarely worked. In fact, once the music really got rockin, they would usually finish their Margaritas and high tail it out of there.

The bar itself was pretty scrungy. Gary hadn't redecorated, or even painted since the early seventies. He opened right after the law was passed allowing the sale of mixed drinks in Lubbock. Lubbock used to be the largest dry city in the country. It sure ain't dry no more! I guess since his patrons were mostly drinking and always in there at night, it didn't really matter how pretty it was. In spite of the atmosphere the place was always packed. Gary said it was us, The Desperados, bringing them in, but I think he was just being nice. We'd partied there ourselves when we weren't playing, and it was still standing room only. Gary was a sweet guy. He was this big old bear, bald, chubby, around sixty. His wife had died about ten years ago, and since then the bar was his whole life. He never had kids, his family were the students that came here, and he loved them and cared for them like they were his own, not just his customers. Gary made sure no one got hurt. He was big on taking car keys if someone had too much to drink, and he was even known to drive someone home himself if a cab couldn't come. He also never liked to see women drunk. He never had a lady's night when women would drink for a buck, and he would stop serving women much sooner than men. He may have been called a chauvinist, but he never wanted to hear the next morning that some girl got hurt because she left Gary's drunk. I respected him for that.

One night, in early May, we had just finished playing our set and ended with this new song I had just written. It brought the house down. It was called "You Can't Get There from Here" and went like this:

Always knew what I wanted; my future seemed so clear.
I'd work real hard for the American Dream-a family and career.
When those would come who'd whisper some temptation in my ear,
I'd just say no 'cause I knew you can't get there from here.

You can't climb the highest mountains,
If you're dancin' on the ground.
You can't build a strong house,
If your foundation isn't sound.
It's easier to give in, if acceptance is your fear,
But conforming never is the way; you can't get there from here.

Now those who used to tempt me, are asking for advice.
They're unhappy with their choices, and how they lived their lives.
They say they're at the bottom as they chug another beer.
Tell'um I won't preach, you know the way, and you can't get there from here.

You can't climb the highest mountains,
If you're dancin' on the ground.
You can't build a strong house,
If your foundation isn't sound.
It's easier to give in, if acceptance is your fear.
But conforming never is the way; you can't get there from here.

So, the guys and me were sitting back, chillin waiting to start the last set. This guy came over to the table and asked if he could sit down. He was dressed in nice clothes, much too nice for a place like Gary's. He kind of looked like a slicker dressed to go to a golf club, not a seedy bar. He had the polo shirt and Dockers thing going on, instead of the jeans and tee shirt thing we all had. We knew he wasn't from around these parts.

"Let me first tell you guys I get asked to come to a lot of these places to see bar bands and I usually decline, but Gary is an old friend, and when he said I needed to hear you guys, I listened. That last song was amazing. Who wrote those lyrics?"

"That would be me," I said.

9

"I am a music agent and I work out of Nashville. Son, I listen to songs all day long. So many that I get to the point where I can't stand to hear another note. Boy, if you've got more songs like that in your head, you're gonna have one hell of a career! What's your name?" He asked.

"I'm Chris. Chris Steele. I don't think I caught your name." I extended my hand to him and gave his a good shake.

"I'm Cyrus Rush. You can call me Cy."

"Thank you, Cy, that's sure nice of you to say that. I just write what I feel."

"Well, keep feeling that way boy, you've got something special. What you could use is a little more edge. I have a feeling that life will have its way of taking care of that. Right now, you're what, nineteen, twenty? Once you get a few more years under your belt and mud on your wheels, you'll be writing with the greats. I can see that."

Man, my head was spinning! I was embarrassed he was saying this to me in front of my band, but they just sat there real quiet, listening to all he said, and when he left the table, I could see they had changed. All of a sudden now I wasn't just their buddy. I had somehow been transformed into the embodiment of their own hopes and dreams. We normally joked around and teased each other, but I had a sense that they were almost trying purposely to be nice to me as if I might take what this guy said to heart and dump my friends because I now have confirmed "talent." I'm not like that. I wouldn't turn my back on my friends. If this guy was right and I make it someday, these guys at the table would be right there with me through the good times. I would never be the kind of guy who turns his back on his friends. I wanted to tell the guys that, but I thought they might think I was starting to get a swelled head if I mentioned anything else about what Cy said, so I just kept my mouth shut which was hard to do since my jaw was still on the floor.

Ted Chapter 3

"I would rather sit on a pumpkin and have it all to myself, than be crowded on a velvet cushion." Henry David Thoreau

There is a certain amount of pragmatism you learn growing up on a one-hundred-acre farm. You learn that to get what you want like food and shelter, you have to treat things well, so they will serve you later on. You cannot just throw some seeds on the ground and expect to come back two months later and have something edible. You must tend to your garden if you hope to reap its fruits.

The same thing is true with livestock. They must be nurtured and tended to everyday up to slaughter day. We slaughtered our own cows and pigs for meat. To this day I can remember my dad telling me to never look at the cow's eyes, because if you ever let yourself get lost in those big brown soulful eyes you will never be able to kill it. After all, they were put on this earth only to serve one need, we shouldn't think of them as a pet or develop any feelings for them. I made that mistake with one of the cows. It was this beautiful cocoa-colored cow that had these deep brown eyes. I chose it as my special cow. I tried not to let anyone know that it was my favorite, but I guess my father noticed I spent more than the normal time with this cow brushing it and petting it. I remember one slaughter day, I was about ten years old, he handed me the gun and made me shoot my cow right between the eyes. He wouldn't let me leave the barn as my older brothers butchered it even though I threw up into a nearby haystack several times. The worst part came later that week when he insisted I eat the meat from my cow, which I also promptly threw up. He followed it with the admonition that I should never get that attached to a cow again.

In spite of this, there were fun times on the farm. We had food on the table, and we had each other. There really couldn't have been much more out there. The only thing we were short on was privacy, but the need for privacy doesn't become important until you are hitting puberty. Then all of a sudden one hundred acres seem quite crowded. I can remember some family dinners when there was so much noise and confusion that I would just have to run outside. I needed to feel the cold air drying the sweat that had formed all over my skin making me feel hot and clammy. My heart would be racing and my head pounding. I just needed to get some space for a little while, and then I always felt better. My siblings teased me about it, but I always made some excuse like I forget to put water out for the cat, or I thought I heard the barn door fly open. I guess they weren't buying it, because they teased me anyway.

My mom wanted us to see another side of life so at age eleven she sent each of us to stay with our aunt in Boston for a year. She felt being exposed to city life would be good for us. I found the kids there were kind of soft and I guess I became a bit of a bully. I did learn from one kid that you can't push too hard, because you might get pushed back. This crazy fat kid almost killed me. My Mom brought me back to the farm sooner than planned. I disliked the city because there were too many people there and they didn't seem to live by the same survival of the fittest rules I grew up with.

When I came back I was allowed to run around the farm with a little more freedom. I used to love to go hiking in the 'back forty' as we used to call it of our one hundred acres. During the summer when school was out, I would rush though my chores so I could have the afternoon to do whatever I wanted, which usually was to just do nothing. I would flop down in the tall green grass and watch the clouds drift by for hours and hours. I was too far away for any of my siblings to find me, and too far to hear my mom call me for dinner. It was just the sunshine and me. Those were the days I loved the most. My siblings and I played all kinds of sports, but sometimes I just craved the solitary indulgence of taking a book with me on my hiking excursions. I guess I was ahead of my time.

Most of my stressed-out executive friends today crave down time now that we are approaching middle age and have families and careers and pressure up the yin/yang. I knew back then that down time was a good thing.

When I reached high school age, my lazy hazy crazy days were numbered. I had to get a job at the local grocery store to help out the family, plus I was in school, plus I had chores to do. This left precious little time to spend doing nothing. The only way I could justify my excursions to the fields was to bring along whatever the latest book was that I had to read for school. I found this actually made the excursions that much more enjoyable. One teacher I had in 11th grade handed us each a copy of Walden by Henry David Thoreau. It didn't look like the kind of thing I would enjoy reading. I was a big science fiction fan, and this didn't seem like there was any story or plot, so I couldn't see it making very good back forty reading.

It was a Friday in April when I suddenly realized I was supposed to read this book by Monday, and I hadn't even started it. I had to work at the grocery store Friday night and Saturday night, which meant I had some time Saturday during the day to read it. Maybe if I just skimmed it, I could get the gist of it, and that would be good enough for me to carry on a conversation about it on Monday. I was a pretty quick study.

Saturday morning after I did all my chores, I headed out to the back forty with book in hand and not much hope in my heart. It was very early spring and still quite chilly, but the sun was doing its best to warm things up. I trudged through the mushy undergrowth, took a shortcut through what would soon be the pumpkin patch, and found a nice spot near this pond that had somehow formed years ago in the back woods.

That pond always fascinated me. When I was really little it wasn't there, then one year dad had plans to build another house that my Uncle would buy and live in with my aunt. He had some builder come and start the project, but he only got as far as digging the cellar when he got into this big argument with dad overpaying him for the job. The guy walked off and left this huge gaping hole. My uncle and aunt ended up getting a divorce and dad was left with this pit in the back. It didn't stay empty for long. That summer happened to have been a very rainy one, and the hole filled up with water. Each summer the water got higher and higher and spread more and more. It would probably be considered more of a puddle than a pond, but I still felt drawn to it. One thing about the pond always fascinated me. Where did the frogs and turtles come from? Over the years frogs and turtles took up residence in the pond. Where did they come from? They weren't there when it was just a field. They didn't fall in with the rain, but there were frogs and turtles living in the pond.

So, there I was with just a few hours to acquaint myself with Mr. Thoreau. I brought a highlighter pen with me just in case I had to highlight something important. Once I started reading it, I started whipping out that highlighter pen at almost every paragraph. Everything I read made sense to me and I could relate to it from every angle. There was one quote in particular that jumped out at me. He said,

"I would rather sit on a pumpkin and have it all to myself, than be crowded on a velvet cushion."

That quote really grabbed my impressionable teenage mind. I really would rather sit on a pumpkin and be alone than have to share my cushion with anyone. Here was a guy one hundred and fifty years ago doing the same thing I longed to do. He left the town and built a little cabin in the woods where he lived alone for two years. I really hoped I could do that someday, or at least something like that. I wanted to be courageous enough to decide to just do nothing, and do it alone. It seemed like a wild concept to a teenage boy, but as I got older, married, life got complicated, it seemed more and more like a great idea.

My farm boy pragmatism got even more finely tuned as I started thinking about my future career. All I wanted out of life was to get a good job that didn't require me to put forth too much effort, and just be able to get married and have children who would take care of me in my old age. That was my plan. I was a math whiz and went on to major in computer science. I got a great job right out of school with this huge computer company in Westchester County, NY. Here I was this farm kid from Columbia County, probably one of the poorest counties in New York state, now living in Westchester, one of the most affluent. I felt like I had made it to the big time. A lot of my friends from school aspired to make it in New York City, but I could never see myself there. It was too crowded and congested for my taste. I visited it with my sister Sally once, and once was enough. I felt like I was suffocating from all the people and noise and concrete. Westchester had enough open spaces to make me feel at ease and comfortable. I was off the farm, I had my own little apartment, and for the first time ever, I had my own stuff. I spent so much time sharing everything I owned with my siblings, that I never really thought about how wonderful it would be to actually own my own things. There was nobody borrowing my clothes, my car, or my money. Everything I had was all mine. I wasn't rich, but it sure felt that way. I no longer had my beloved back forty, but I had control of the remote and I could eat whatever I wanted to for dinner. I had the life. Now I needed to work on part two of my plan.

Billy Chapter 4

I had earned a bit of respect and fear after the incident on the bus and no one bothered with me. The next few years I channeled my energies into sports, and although I often was ejected from games for having a bad attitude, or fighting with a coach or referee, I still loved playing. Sports melted the baby fat, and I was a good-looking guy underneath the layers of fat I shed. I looked forward to my college days so I could move away from home and have a fresh start. I went to college in New Jersey near where my Grandmother and Great Grandmother lived. I missed the Hub. I had to learn a new language, like they call grinders subs down here, but I could get used to it. I figured I could have some time on my own, but still be close to a family member if I ever really went off the deep end. What I discovered was that being on my own meant I had to live with the worst roommate possible...me. I really hated being by myself. I had to constantly referee the two sides of my personality. I was always trying to hide Mr. Bad from everyone so that I could at least attempt to appear normal. I did all this, I am sure, on an unconscious level for I do not recall ever having this internal dialog. One thing was for sure, I did not want to stay alone forever.

I became very close to Granny and my great grandmother whom I called Nonna. I would stop at their house a few times a week, usually when I was hungry or needed my laundry done. I was a typical college kid in that respect. Granny was a neat freak who did laundry better than anyone on the planet. She even ironed socks. Nonna cooked like a pro. She was in her nineties, but man was she sharp! She was full of life, and agile and just fun to be around. I tried to repay them by being the pseudo-man around the house, mowing the lawn, fixing things and opening tight jars. It was a symbiotic relationship.

One of the best and worst experiences of my life happened on the same day. My Grandmother died, and I met Lucy. Granny slipped and fell on an icy patch and never regained consciousness. I had grown extremely close to her that past year, I was shattered. The shock of having her here one minute and gone the next was just something I could not believe. The onslaught of neighbors and friends and relatives coming over to comfort the family was terribly overwhelming. I was not quite used to such displays of affection. Growing up in New England, we are a bit less demonstrative, so the whole grieving-in-public process left me a bit flustered.

People were coming by with trays and trays of cookies and cakes and sandwiches and food. There were so many people in the house I could barely breathe. Then a breath of fresh air swept through the door. A neighbor and her daughter came in with yet another cake. I vaguely recognized the woman as a friend of my mother's, but the daughter took my breath away. It was my Lucy. I knew from the moment I saw her that she was going to be in my life forever.

Sad to say I almost forgot where I was, and the circumstances and tried to make a play for her. I wasn't very smooth or suave, heck I was only nineteen at the time, but something in me saw the faces of my unborn children telling me to go after this girl and not take no for an answer.

We chatted and found out we were the same age and both in college. She wanted to be a writer and was studying journalism at Monmouth State College. I was studying philosophy but thinking I might switch to pre-law. Her very long brown hair was pulled back into a high, off centered ponytail. She wore no make-up, just a deep crimson lipstick that made her full luscious lips look like some delectable forbidden fruit that I had to have a taste of. She was pretty but in a natural way. She didn't seem to know it either which made her even more attractive. The conversation was easy and fun. I often forgot that my mother and Nonna were in the next room in deep mourning. Lucy did not forget however and offered to take my great-grandmother on a trip to Atlantic City to cheer her up. I thought that was an incredibly noble gesture, but as I got to know Lucy, I learned that those were the kind of things she did routinely without even thinking about it. She was a self-sacrificing, generous woman. It was one of the things I loved most about her, and I tortured her for it.

Lucy Chapter 5

"In the long-run men hit only what they aim at, therefore, though they should fail immediately, they had better aim at something high." Henry David Thoreau

Rico was always getting into mischief, not real trouble, just mischief. He bought a Harley as soon as he was old enough to. His motorcycle club became his extended family, and I was an extended part of theirs, which meant I was vicariously protected from harm by forty or fifty big burly bikers who treated me like their own little sister. Rico was not your typical biker, he marched to his own beat. We grew up loving books. He was always sneaking away to read a book and I am sure he took a lot of ribbing from his friends because of it. It shocked my parents when he decided not to go to college, but instead kept working at a garage as a mechanic. I think it especially hurt my mom who was always telling us how her biggest regret in life was not finishing college.

I went to a local college because my, overly protective, antiquely strict parents would not allow me to go away. It was okay with me because I was not into partying and hanging out in bars anyway. I was able to spend my free time doing what I loved to do which was writing and not have to bother with roommates dragging me out to parties or guys trying to make me their latest conquest. My little cocoon world was cozy and safe with Gestapo parents controlling me, and Hell's Guardian Angels protecting me.

My mother patiently cared for my elderly Grandmother, lovingly feeding her, and bathing her when she became too old and feeble to care for herself. I always felt she had taken a very noble course. She did it without complaint and looked for no thanks other than the satisfaction of knowing she was fulfilling her daughterly obligation. At least that is how it appeared to me. My Grandma passed away when I was a teenager and my dad's mom had died before I was born. I vaguely remember my paternal grandfather who died when I was five, and my maternal grandfather left my grandmother when she was pregnant with their sixth child, so needless to say he was dead to the family as well. So, there I was in my late teens orphaned by all grandparents and in desperate need of an elderly person in my life to care for me and that I could care for. My own parents had me when they were quite young and are only in their forties, which hardly qualify, as elderly. I have no old aunts or uncles. I truly felt I was missing a link to the past and needed to fill that void.

Then came Mrs. Rinaldi. Mrs. Rinaldi was an elderly woman who lived on the next block. I never really thought of her as old because she was spry and lively. I used to see her everyday walking around the block. I would always acknowledge her, but rarely stopped to talk to her or hear her stories. I remember knocking on her door at Halloween when I was little. Some of the old people in the neighborhood would give those horrible little wrapped candies that looked like strawberries. Nobody ever eats them, but everybody has them in their candy dish. Others would give unwrapped lemon drops. You learned to avoid those houses. Not Mrs. Rinaldi, she always gave full size Snickers bars, not those itty-bitty snack size ones, full size! I never told any of the other kids about the full sized Snickers for fear that it would get all over town and then poor Mrs. Rinaldi would not have enough money to buy those big bars, and would have to close her door to trick-or-treaters. I kept it as my little secret.

For years Mrs. Rinaldi's daughter lived with her. She shopped for her, cooked for her, and cared for her every need. Her daughter was around 70 years old and had been widowed a few years ago. She had two daughters and one grandson. One family lived in Boston and the other about an hour away and I only recall seeing them when there was a holiday.

The winter of '82 was a horrible one on the east coast. There was snowstorm after snowstorm with no let up. Everything was icy and slippery and cold that winter. It was January and I was off for my winter recess, and thought I should probably check in on Mrs. Rinaldi just to make sure she didn't need anything, but then I felt she had her daughter there, so there really wasn't a pressing need to.

I will never forget the night my mother told me the news. We were sitting around at dinner, mom, my dad, me and Rico, when my mom said she was going to bring a cake over to Mrs. Rinaldi. Now Mom is known to be sweet like that, but she looked like there was another reason so I, inquisitive soul, asked "Why?"

"Her daughter passed away today."

Sadness and confusion hit at the same time. "How, Mom? She wasn't sick"

"She took a fall this morning on the ice and hit her head. She never regained consciousness.

"Oh, how awful!" I was horrified. I couldn't imagine anything more frightening than to think you could be walking along fine and healthy one minute and dead the next. Then the thought hit me that if it was unfathomable to me, how must it be for poor Mrs. Rinaldi, she just lost her daughter? "I'll come with you to deliver the cake mom." I threw my hair up in a pony, put on my favorite lipstick, grabbed my coat and we were out the door.

It was still snowing. It fell so silently that winter. The streets were dark and cold and quiet. When you looked at the streetlights you could see the fine snow swirling around the light like a living snow globe. It was as if life was suspended for a few hours while the earth took a white shower. I held the plastic cake carrier in one hand and held Mom's arm with the other. Even though Mom seemed annoyed at my cautiousness, she's virtually Eatontown's Queen of Tai-bo and in great physical shape, the thought of what had just happened to Mrs. Rinaldi's daughter made every step seem dangerous, this snow was a silent killer just waiting to claim its next victim, and I wasn't going to let that next victim be my Mom.

We crossed the street and headed towards Johnson Road where Mrs. Rinaldi lived. There were many people at the house a few of which I vaguely recognized as her grandchildren. My mom went up to a plump woman about her age blotting red puffy eyes with a tissue that should have been tossed long ago. In the other hand she held a chicken leg that she was consoling herself with.

"Fran, I am so sorry, what a horrible shock" said mom as she set the cake down next to about seven others on a table that looked like it was being set up for a high school bake sale. "How is Grandma taking it?"

"Very badly. She hasn't spoken to any of us. She keeps chanting 'my beautiful daughter, where is my beautiful daughter?' It's really sad. "You were so sweet to come, Jen. And how are you, Lucy?" She asked once she realized I was there.

"I'm fine, Fran, I am just so sorry to hear about your mother. Please, if there is anything I can do for you or your Grandmother, let me know."

As if I were not in the room she replied to mom, "Jen, you have a very sweet daughter. She is so much like you when you were younger." My mom and Fran grew up together. They went to the same high school and had been friends for a long time. I did, however, hear mom pass a few comments about how little time Fran spent with her grandmother and mother lately. She lived in Boston, but mom felt that it shouldn't be that much of an effort to spend time with your elders.

"How are Billy and Dorothy taking it?" Asked mom. Billy was Fran's son and Dorothy her sister.

"Billy is devastated, and Dorothy is running around trying to organize everything, acting like a drill sergeant. I am worried about Billy. He got very close to his Grandmother this past year. He's in college down here and spent a lot of time with them.

I remember Billy; in fact, I had a crush on him when I was about thirteen. He was visiting his grandmother and I had been over at their house with my mom. He didn't know I was even in the room, but I had a crush on him. I wondered if he was still cool and mysterious.

"Billy, come here, I want you to say hello to someone." I turned around and saw Billy and my heart started flopping around in my chest. He was better looking than I had remembered. His dark, wavy hair was shorter and very stylish. He was wearing jeans and a solid cream-colored Quiana button down shirt, which gave him a very casual, but decidedly comfortable look. You could tell he had been crying. His dark brown eyes were puffy underneath, and his nose was red from being blown too many times. He looked much older than nineteen and for the moment he looked like he needed to be loved.

Fran took Billy's hand and said "Billy, this is my very dear old friend Jen and her daughter Lucy, you must remember them from Nonna's neighborhood." He gave my mom a very polite smile, and then looked at me and his face seemed to brighten up…unless it was my imagination.

"Little Lucy from the next block? No suh, you've grown up! I haven't seen you since we were kids…you're all…grown up"!

So, he did remember me. He had the cutest Boston accent. Mom and Fran moved into the kitchen to tend to some desserts and Billy and I remained talking in the living room. Even though there were tons of people around, it seemed like we were the only two people in the room, in fact, in the world. He was someone I felt instantly comfortable with. He seemed vulnerable, yet confident at the same time. Almost like two different people. "I am so sorry about your grandmother. It must have been such a shock."

"It was. My Grandma and I became very close this past year. I practically lived here. She spoiled me rotten. She was always there for me, and I don't think I can ever forgive myself for not being here when she died."

"But Billy it happened so fast; you couldn't have known."

"I think she knew. Granny always had premonitions. She had asked me to come over yesterday to spend some time with her and Nonna, but I told her I was too busy. I don't even know what I had to do that was so important. I can't believe I blew off seeing my grandma for the last time, because I had to study or something equally dumb. How stupid is that?"

"But you didn't know it was going to be the last time." I said.

"You never know when it's going to be the last time." He answered quite astutely.

"That's true." I paused for a moment to try to come up with something deep and profound to say. I couldn't think of anything, so I countered with the first thought to come to my mind "Are you hungry?"

"Yes, I've been so busy talking with people that I really haven't eaten. Come on, there's this huge table of food in the parlor."

I followed him into the room that I would have called a living room, its' table a sea of Tupperware. My mom's cake had been moved in from the dessert oasis by the door where it was placed when we first walked in.

"Would you like a grinder, I mean a sub?" He asked.

"Oh, no thanks, I just had dinner, I will have a piece of cake, though." I always had a sweet tooth and situations like this were no different.

"Good for you! I am so sick of the girls at school who won't go near sweets or desserts because they're afraid to put on an ounce. You obviously have nothing to worry about, you look great."

I was not sure if I was hearing him correctly. If I did not know he was in mourning, I would swear he was coming on to me. I just managed to smile and say thank you. I was not used to getting compliments. I'm just an average looking girl, and I have never had a boyfriend, or even a boy pay this much attention to me. It felt right and awkward at the same time.

Mrs. Rinaldi came into the room and I wanted to offer to do something for her beyond the usual general 'if there is anything I can do, please let me know' kind of thing. I remember my mom saying Mrs. Rinaldi loved to go to Atlantic City with her senior's club. I thought I could drive her down there some Saturday.

"Mrs. Rinaldi when you are feeling better we'll take a trip to Atlantic City and have a fun day in the casino." Her face totally lit up.

"Well, my senior citizen's club is having an outing next month, I can get tickets for us to go." Even though this was something she loved to do I half expected that she would want to wait a few more months until the shock of her daughter's death wore off before she would want to go. I was mistaken. Well, I guess if it could take her mind off what she has just gone through, I did not mind doing it.

"Oh, but I don't mind driving you some Saturday. It's not far. Only about an hour."

"Nonsense! The trip with the club is three weeks from Thursday and they give vouchers back for $17 in coins! Why should you have to take your car?"

I did not want to get into the million reasons why I would rather drive than take the bus, not the least of which was that I would have to miss class for a whole day to do this. "You're right, the bus trip sounds like fun. We'll plan it."

"Thank you, Lucy, that will be a nice thing to look forward to. I haven't been able to go in so long because of my bad arthritis. My beautiful daughter couldn't go with me because the cigarette smoke was bad for her asthma. I was afraid to go by myself. We will have a nice day." As she left the room to tend to some new visitors she added, "Have some baked ziti, Mrs. Maloney sent it over" Then she leaned in closer to me and whispered "It's sauce from a jar...she's Irish you know..." She left Billy and me alone again.

"Wow, that was some offer! I would rather be in hell than on a bus to a casino with forty old biddies. You are one brave soul." He said.

"Where's your sense of adventure? It will be fun. I'm sure they have some really great stories to tell." I answered.

"And tell, and tell, and tell...."

"You're terrible!" I said in a mock shock voice.

"And you're wonderful" He said in a soft, sweet and sincere voice. I just blushed and subtly changed the subject. I was at once feeling both excited, and uncomfortable. I was not sure if this was a great feeling or an awful one. I was finding that I liked him, but something about the timing just did not feel right. He just lost his grandmother, should he be coming on to me right now? Maybe he gets it from his great-grandmother. She just lost a daughter and yet she was able to just plan a trip to the casino. I guess some people deal with grief differently than others.

Rico Chapter 6

My folks were strict with us when we were kids, but as I got older, and they did too, I started to wear them down and get away with a lot of crap. I felt bad for Lucy because she never fought back and always tried to do exactly what they told her to do. I used to tell her she would have more fun if she took a walk on the wild side every now and then. She took a different route. While still in college she married Billy and five minutes later was knocked up with my baby niece Olivia. A year later, my little man Joey came. I love her and I love those kids, but all I wanted to do was ride motorcycles. I wasn't ready to settle in one place yet when there were so many places to see. My brother-in law Billy is a couple of years younger than me and he's already got the weight of the world on his shoulders with a wife and two kids. They seem happy, though. I never see Sister Sunshine without a big smile on her face. Billy, well, he works a lot, so I just never see him.

I pumped gas and fixed cars in a station off the Parkway and another one near the shore putting in like eighty hours a week until I had enough money to buy my first Harley. It belonged to this old biker dude, Richie, who was leaving this motorcycle club, The Desperations. I was barely twenty years old and didn't know who The Desperations were or even what a motorcycle club was. He had just turned fifty and his old lady didn't want him riding anymore. I can't see myself ever letting anybody tell me what to do. He almost cried when he handed me the papers for that bike. He looked so defeated; you could see it on his face. I felt sorry for the guy, but man, that bike was sweet. The guy kept it like mint. I loved older bikes and this one was perfect. It was a 1976 Harley Sportster with a fresh coat of 1000cc gloss black paint, electric start ignition, all chromed out with a new mirror, new 2" drag pipes, new carburetor, and new tires.

I didn't set out to be in a motorcycle club it just happened. Shortly after I got the bike I started hanging out with The Desperations. They looked mean, but most were normal guys. There may have been a felon or two in the group, but no more than you would find in church on any given Sunday. You don't just join one of these things, you have to be accepted. You have to prove that you can ride well, and you would lay your life down for one of your brothers in the club. I was kinda the golden boy in the club. I was asked to join because I took a knife for the president of the club, Nicky.

It was a few years ago after I had bought the bike from Richie. Me and my buddy John were down at a dive near Seaside having a couple of beers when we hear the thunder of about twenty bikes pulling up. These real tough-ass looking guys and girls come in wearing leather and denim. I had on jeans and a denim jacket because it was early May and I thought it was too warm for leather. Apparently, these guys didn't think so. Tattoos covered most of their exposed body parts, and a lot of them had a shaved head except for a tuft of hair going from their forehead down to the back of their necks like a Mohawk. On their backs they all had the same big patch that had a skull head with arrows sticking through it and a Mohawk haircut. On the front of their jackets or vests as if it was a military uniform, they had their rank. I saw one that said 'president', one that said, 'vice president', there was a 'sergeant-at-arms', a 'general', a 'lieutenant' and then there were a bunch that said 'pledge'. I admit, when you see them for the first time you think you're about to be killed.

Me and John weren't looking for no trouble that night, so we quickly downed our beers and were going to book it out of there. This guy comes up to us as we are trying to leave, our leather boots gave us away as riders. You have to wear them when riding or else you'll break a foot or something. I thought he was going to kick our asses for being in his territory. Instead he asked, "Who's got the '76 Sportster out there?"

My heart was smacking itself so hard against my chest wall I thought it was trying to break out. I was sure I was about to get killed for being in the wrong place at the wrong time. I thought of how my mom would take the news that I was killed because of a bike. She was sure I was going to kill myself on it, but not just because I owned it. This guy was about forty-five years old. His black hair was splattered with gray and in a buzz cut, six silver stud earrings lining one ear and six small silver hoops on the other. He had tattoos up and down his arm and fresh ink on the back of his right hand that said "Richie" I noticed the guys' rank. He was the frickin president. It figures I had to piss off the president of these thugs. John was just hanging back minding his own business with a look on his face that said, 'I feel sorry for you man, but I'm glad he's talking to you and not me.' I hated him for looking like such a coward.

I finally got the nerve up to say, "I do."

The guy says, "You bought that from Richie Keith?"

"Yeah."

"He's my brother."

The guy started looking like a regular guy and not some kind of monster. "Oh yeah?" was the best I could squeeze out of my throat. The band had just come back from their break, so it was getting loud in there again.

"You got the other bike out there?" This time the question was directed to John and I felt slightly relieved that he was now in the hot seat.

"Yeah, that's mine" He said trying to sound tough.

"Your rear tire's a little low, be careful." John and I shot each other a look like we must have imagined this guy just said that. The guy was around my father's age, and he's giving us safety tips? Two minutes ago, we thought the Angel of Death rode in on his Harley, and he turns out to be a big teddy bear.

"Come outside with me for a minute, I can't hear myself think over this shitty music" the guy said. The band was lousy. They were trying to cover Springsteen and failing miserably at it. All bar bands in Jersey try to cover Springsteen; they just never quite seem to understand there's only one Boss.

We followed him out the door. The sergeant-at-arms followed us. This guy was built like a tank with a totally shaved head. He had a denim vest on with the club's colors on the back. He was probably about forty years old. He looked like the kind of guy you would see by day on a road crew working a jackhammer. He didn't say anything to us but was watching every move we made. You knew he was there to protect the other guy.

The president guy offered us a cigarette and took one himself. As soon as he put it to his lips the sergeant-at-arms whipped out a lighter and lit it up for him. He didn't offer us the same service. The guy took a long drag on his cigarette, then with the smoke sailing out his mouth he extended his hand to shake mine, then John's. "I'm Nicky," he said.

"Rico," I said as he shook my hand.

"John," said my buddy as he did the same.

"Where you guys from?" He asked.

"Eatontown," I answered for both of us. The whole time his eyes never left my bike.

There was silence for a few moments as he finished his cigarette and flicked it into the gravel driveway. Then he spoke. "The day my brother sold you that bike was the worst day of his life." He said with this far off look on his face.

"Does he want it back?" I asked.

"He died two weeks ago."

I didn't know what to say. Here was this guy that most people, myself included, would run from, and now he was a human in mourning. All of a sudden, I was seeing this guy as a normal guy who probably had a wife and kids, and a mother and father and widowed sister-in-law that he spends Christmas and Thanksgiving with. I learned a lot that night about judging people on their appearance. "Oh, man, I'm so sorry."

"He had cancer, that's one of the reasons why his wife wanted him to quit riding. She didn't want to lose him any sooner than she was already going to, but not riding seemed to take the life right out of him."

I didn't know what to say so we just stood there in the parking lot for a while having another cigarette. I was remembering the day I bought the bike. Having met Nicky, I could see the resemblance between the two brothers. I understood the tears in Richie's eyes. He wasn't just losing his bike; he was losing his life as well.

"I gotta take a pee boss," said the sergeant-at-arms.

He disappeared behind the building just as these two drunk bikers pull up wearing different colors. It all happened so fast. They see Nicky's colors and say in a slurred accent. "Death to The Desperations" I look down and realize one has a knife and he's about to plunge it into Nicky's back. I tackled Nicky like I used to tackle the opposing quarterbacks back in high school, only unlike my high school football career, this time I succeeded. The guys just got back on their bikes and rode away laughing and whooping it up like wild Indians from some bad old cowboy movie. The sergeant-at-arms comes running over, still pulling up the zipper on his jeans. John was trying to get us up.

"Oh my God, Rico, man, you're bleeding!" I heard John say. I heard the sergeant-at-arms tell John to go inside and call the ambulance.

"Nicky, Nicky are you okay?" The sergeant at arms was afraid to move me so Nicky was still under me. Eventually, I was able to roll off him, but my arm was burning like fire. I wasn't even sure it was still a part of my body. I heard Nicky say he was okay, just knocked out for a minute, and I heard him talking to me, but I don't remember what he said before I passed out.

Next thing I remember was waking up in the emergency room of Bayshore Community Hospital. Nicky and John were next to me. Nicky had bandages going around his chest that I could see from under his vest. "I cracked a rib when you tackled me, but you saved my life. How's your arm?" Nicky asked.

"It hurts like hell. Is it still there?"

"Yeah, you had to get 64 stitches, and you'll have one hell of a pretty scar, but you'll be fine," said Nicky.

"Did they catch the guys?" I asked.

"Four of our guys took off after them and caught them about five miles from where it went down. They beat the shit out of them, and I think they are two or three rooms down from here. Stupid bastards. It's this group of riders who don't want to do nothing but cause trouble. They give bikers like us a bad name." I saw the humor in Nicky's statement, but I thought since I didn't know him that well and my head really hurt, I shouldn't laugh. "You saved my life," he repeated, "I'll never forget that." I could tell he was sincere. "You're in the club, no initiation, nothing. I just want you riding with me."

"Thank you," was all I could manage to say. I knew he felt as though he was bestowing a great honor on me, but I was in too much pain to react to the monumental significance of his offer.

So that is how I became a member of The Desperations. I asked Nicky to let John join too, and since he liked me so much, he agreed. Sometimes, when we could all get some time off from work, me and John and some of the guys from the club would ride down to Wildwood on Sunday mornings, but during the week bikers lead pretty normal lives. They run their own businesses like deli's or car washes, or body shops, but on weekends, they put on their colors and ride. They usually don't wear their colors unless they're going out together. You won't see one lone guy walking down the street on a Tuesday afternoon with his colors on, it ain't happening. You will see seven or eight of them on a Friday night at the local diner or beer joint. They are family guys, and a lot of their wives ride with them. There are a lot of single guys who ride with girls. The girls are hot. Usually they are very smart, rich girls who are looking for some excitement and to piss off their Daddies. Nothing gets an old man's blood boiling like seeing his little princess with her arms wrapped around some big smelly dude on a Harley. And man, we are smelly! It's a combo of cigarette smoke, leather in need of a cleaning, gasoline, and hit or miss hygiene.

I liked riding with the club. The guys all treated me like a brother from the first time I rode with them, partly because I saved Nicky, and partly because they are just good guys. If one of us gets hurt or sick or is in trouble, we all rally around helping the family, making sure the kids are okay. Nobody ever is alone again once they join the club. The stories about wild parties and orgies are mostly myth. In fact, I remember my mom having Tupperware parties that were raunchier than most of the biker parties I've been to. They drink, but they don't get too wasted. They don't sip cocktails; they have shots of one of the boys, Jim, Jack, or José. They rarely drink to the point of falling down drunk, because they know they rode in alone, and are going to have to ride home alone. You can't hitch a ride home with somebody if you're too drunk to hold on, and nobody wants to drop their bike, so you don't ride if you're drunk. There are a lot of unwritten rules that everybody follows.

Lucy Chapter 7

I spent a great deal of time with Mrs. Rinaldi after her daughter's death. I would stop by her house every afternoon after school to check in on her. If she needed anything from the store, I would get it for her. Sometimes I would stay and have dinner with her. That was a treat. She was a wonderful cook. So was my mom, but Mrs. Rinaldi really could have owned a restaurant!

She would cry, but it would come in sudden bursts, last for just a few seconds, and then she would be off on the next topic again. Sometimes I could not keep up with how quickly her moods would change. I would try, but I always found that this 91-year-old lady was leaving me in the dust. We would talk about food and her family and all the friends she has, and those that have gone. She would tell me about some of her family scandals in a whisper and tell of the triumphs with great pride. She was ridiculously hard of hearing and compensated for it by just not letting anybody get a word in edgewise. When I was in Mrs. Rinaldi's presence I just listened. It was as if she just needed to have someone in front of her to tell her stories to. I didn't mind, she had so many to tell, she didn't repeat her repertoire, and they really were enjoyable stories.

One story she told a lot though was the story of Billy. He was her pride and joy. He was the baby of the family and the only male. This gave him extra points in her book. He had great promise. He was going to a very good college, was at the top of his class and headed to law school. "I just wish he could find a nice girl. Do you have a boyfriend, Lucy?"

Her subtlety could use a little work. I would usually change the subject back to food or something when she would hint like that. I did find Billy very attractive, but I really didn't need to get involved with anyone now.

We talked about the approach of the trip to the casino and she was very excited thinking about it.   Finally, the day arrived. I got to her house around 7:30am to help her get ready and drive her over to the club where the bus was waiting. She had packed lunch for both of us, eggplant parmigiana sandwiches. I know there are plenty of nice restaurants at the Casino, but this was the way Mrs. Rinaldi wanted to do it.

The trip to the Casino was quite the adventure. I was the only one on the bus who still had my original teeth and had never lived through a war. Most of the people on the bus were at least seventy-five years old or better. When I got on the bus one of the ladies smiled at me and said, "Oh it's so nice to have a beautiful young face going with us!" I smiled back and responded that I thought I was on a bus full of beautiful young ladies. All those who could hear well enough to catch my reply giggled. They were beautiful. Each one of them had lived amazing lives, raised dozens of children, had husbands, many of whom probably did not appreciate them, and treated them with little respect. They had buried parents, spouses, friends, sisters, brothers, and in Mrs. Rinaldi's case, children. They all had stories to tell and I wished I could have stayed on that bus long enough to hear them all.

When Mrs. Rinaldi got on the bus, the ladies all came up to her and offered their condolences for her daughter's passing. She cried a little, but each was quick to point out that they had all experienced death of some sort, and all had made it through. There was a reason why God chose to take her daughter before He took her, and maybe it was because she was going to hit a big jackpot at the Casino. That seemed to make her feel better. It was sweet the way they cared about one another. They knew no amount of money could ever replace losing a daughter, but they were trying to make the point that there was a reason for it, and we should not question God's plan. I guess it takes years of living to finally feel comfortable with that concept. The concept was not lost on Mrs. Rinaldi. She perked right up again. I noticed with her there was no prolonged mourning. She mourned for moments at a time but went about living her life. When something made her sad, she cried. After a few moments she was fine again.

They had the most fascinating jewelry. Not big and expensive, but each piece had a story attached to it. The gold was not the gold we see today. It had a different hue, like it was from another country, and probably was. Their rings slid sideways on their fingers. Too big, perhaps, because they once belonged to some long gone relative, or perhaps because their hands were withered with age, or maybe they were made bigger to accommodate arthritic knuckles. There were bracelets with dangling charms memorializing the story of a birth or a communion or a graduation. Earrings hung on wrinkly ears that once were whispered into by some love long since passed. Their jewelry could talk. They were proud of the history held inside each piece, proud of the slight envy it evoked in the person sitting next to them, and proud of the fact that they could remember the story each bauble had to tell.

I had naively brought along a book to read on the bus, but soon realized that the noise level would make reading impossible, especially something I would have to concentrate on like Thoreau. It was all right, though. I would learn as much by eavesdropping on the conversations that were being carried out in something far more deaf-defying than a whisper.

The chatter on the bus was non-stop. Most on the bus were ladies; there were only two gentlemen of the forty-four passengers—a statistic not unnoticed by the ladies. They were all over those men like nothing I have ever seen before. The more aggressive women were the ones with matching shoes and handbags. I do not know why, they just were! Their flirting was adorable. They always offered food, and the one who had the best sandwich to offer was the one who got the chance to sit with one of the dashing men, or 'the boys' as they called them, instead of one of their tired old sisters.

The other women on the bus knew there was no contest. Mrs. Rinaldi made the best eggplant in all of Eatontown, but she relinquished her chance to sit next to one of the boys so she could sit next to me. "You don't bread the eggplant, just dip it in egg, then fry it, and make sure you buy the male eggplants, they are the ones that are long and thin and don't have too many seeds, the seeds are what make it bitter. You also must *cook* your marinara sauce. Everybody is in such a rush; they don't take the time to let the sauce cook." These were the secrets Mrs. Rinaldi imparted on her delicious eggplant. Having a young person next to you was an envious position, even more than having one of the boys sit next to you. Mrs. Rossi in the third row with her prosciutto and fresh mozzarella won one of the boys, and Mrs. Maloney with her homemade corned beef on rye won the other. Mrs. Maloney sported an emerald green handbag and emerald green loafers.

The group leader on the bus had everyone stop chattering long enough to pray before the bus took off. After all, this was a church club that ran this event. "Gladys will you shut your mouth; we're praying now!" She shouted to the nearly deaf woman in the seventh row. Bless us, oh Lord and keep us safe on this trip, and if any of us win, we will remember it was thanks to You, Lord, and be very generous in Sunday's basket. Amen" I always thought you weren't supposed to pray for money, but I guess if you are offering to put a generous donation in the basket, it's ok.

In the casino I stayed rather close to Mrs. Rinaldi because I know she has bad arthritis, and it is hard for her to put the coins into the machine. I didn't want anyone stealing her purse or anything while she struggled with the coins, so I didn't leave her side the whole time. We had eaten our eggplant sandwiches at 9:30 am on the bus, not my idea of lunchtime, but when in Rome…. I saw a cocktail waitress coming towards us and flagged her down. "I'll have a ginger-ale, and Mrs. Rinaldi what would you like to drink?"

Without moving her eyes from the three spinning wheels in front of her she said, "I'll have a gin and tonic" I nearly fell off my seat.

"Mrs. Rinaldi are you sure you can drink one of those?"

"Sure, a little drink every now and then will never hurt you."

Okay, so I learned something new today. Eating spicy food at 9:30 in the morning and hard liquor before noon was actually good for you. Who could argue with a woman who is in excellent health at ninety-one years old?

We were in the casino for about five hours. I did not bring much money, which was fine since I really didn't have any time on my own to gamble. Mrs. Rinaldi was going through money like it was Monopoly currency. She kept asking me to change hundred-dollar bills into coins for her. I did this at least three times for her. After the first time I started walking very very slowly back to her just so it would stretch her money out. When I would come into view, she would motion for me to walk faster. She could not wait to start putting more money into the machine. I really didn't understand the fascination with this pursuit. If she were winning I suppose that would be another story, but she kept losing. I kept imagining all the things I could buy with the money she was throwing away in this machine, make-up, new clothes, and schoolbooks. I guess none of those things are of any interest to a ninety-one-year-old woman. All she wanted to buy was a chance at hitting a big jackpot and leaving some money to her heirs. This made her a better person than I was. I spend money on things; she spends money on a dream, an unselfish one at that.

It was time to catch the bus. The day went by rather quickly. I asked Mrs. Rinaldi if she enjoyed her day. "I didn't come here to learn anything, just to forget my troubles and pains for a few hours." I guess that was it in a nutshell. The trip to the casino was an escapist thing that let her live a fantasy of being a wealthy woman for a few hours. After what she has just gone through, she deserved a day of fun.

I got on the bus to find the ladies and the "boys" were very tired. I would finally get my chance to read, but when I put my light on in the darkened bus the lady behind me tapped me on the shoulder and said, "Do you mind shutting that light, darling, it hurts my cataracts?"

"No problem." I just sat back in my seat next to a very tired Mrs. Rinaldi and let the bus take us home.

By the time we got back to Eatontown and I drove Mrs. Rinaldi, as well as all the elderly ladies I could fit in my car, it was after 8:00. I walked her in and found Billy there.

"Hello Nonna, Hi Lucy" he said with his infectious smile. I had to smile back. There was something about being with Billy that made me feel really good about myself. I think it was his vulnerability. He had a great sensitivity. He was not a typical macho jerk. I always had the desire to just scoop him up into my arms and hold him until the demons inside him were all chased away. I knew he had a complicated nature and was probably not the best thing for me right now, but I could not help but be almost magnetically drawn to him. I could also see how happy it made Mrs. Rinaldi to see the two of us together. She hinted rather obviously on numerous occasions how all Billy needs is a good woman to straighten him out. He was getting lectures of his own from her I am sure. He seemed to be coming over to see his Nonna a lot more often. I'm not sure if it was as a result of losing his grandmother so suddenly and needing to reconnect with his great-grandmother, or if he was trying to see me. Either way, both were good reasons as far as I was concerned. Billy and I dated for the next year and things were going along great. I really enjoyed being with him. He was so handsome; it made me feel beautiful just to stand next to him. Mrs. Rinaldi and I got closer every day. In fact, she would have me bring her to the club sometimes and she would introduce me to her friends as her granddaughter. Gee, no pressure there! I knew she already saw Billy and I as a done deal, and at this point in time, that wouldn't have bothered me at all.

She started taking out the heavy artillery. One night when Billy and I were over for dinner, she said, "You know, Billy, I am an old woman and don't know when my last day will be, I would love to know before I leave this earth that you are settled down, married, and maybe give me a great-great grandchild..." I saw his face turn pale. I almost dropped the glass I was holding. Then she turned the pressure on to me, "Lucy, you are such a sweet girl, don't you want to settle down and get married some day and have children? You know, time runs out for a woman, you don't want to be having children when you are too old to enjoy them."

"But Mrs. Rinaldi, I'm only twenty."

"By your age I already had my darling daughter, God rest her soul. She was the joy of my life. I would hate to see you miss out on that kind of joy. Well, I am very tired, Lucy, will you please clean up while I go upstairs?"

"Sure, Mrs. Rinaldi, dinner was delicious, thank you." She was about as subtle as a sledgehammer. She was not tired one bit. She planted this thought into our heads and wanted to leave us alone so we could discuss it.

Billy helped me clear the table and we stood by the sink doing dishes for a few moments in silence. Then he spoke. "You know, Lucy, Nonna isn't totally off base here. It's something I've been thinking about for a while." He had such a sweet and soft-spoken way about him that I found totally irresistible.

I chose to act innocent in an annoying fashion. I did not know how to handle what was coming next, so I thought I could joke my way out of it. "So, you think the batteries in my biological clock are going dead too?"

"Stop. That's not what I mean. I mean I've been thinking about getting married, settling down, having kids, the whole nine."

"Great! Who's the lucky girl?"

"Come on, be serious, you know I love you, and you have done so much for me. You have changed every part of me. You have made me rethink my life and who I am, and what is important, and I think now I'm ready to take care of you." He paused for a moment and put the damp dishtowel down and took my wet hands out of the sink. "Lucy, will you marry me?" He pulled an ancient looking jewelry box out of his pocket and inside was the most beautiful antique ring. "Nonna wants you to have her ring. Please say yes!"

Well, he did say please…. "Yes, Billy, I'll marry you!" He held me in this huge bear hug for what seemed like hours. "Should we wake Nonna and tell her the news?"

"I have a feeling she already knows." He walked over to the bottom of the steps and called up," Nonna…you got your wish"

"Oh, Billy, I'm so happy! Lucy, my darling, I am so happy!"

She went off to bed and we left to go share the news with my family. I really did not think I could be happier. I was getting married! I was going to officially be a member of Mrs. Rinaldi's family. I was marrying the love of my life.

Diana Chapter 8

"I went to the woods because I wished to live deliberately, to front only the essential facts of life, and see if I could not learn what it had to teach, and not, when I came to die, discover that I had not lived." Henry David Thoreau.

There was this little bakery around the corner from my house on Brigantine Island in New Jersey that made the most amazing smelling homemade cinnamon buns they called Bismarcks. They were these warm spirals of soft fresh dough swirled with cinnamon, baked to gooey perfection and glazed in sugar. The smell would make my mouth water, but at the same time make me nauseous because I would think how just one of these evil buns would make me fat and then I would get mad at myself for even entertaining the idea of eating one, but oh, the smell! Maybe I could get one some morning, and then spend the rest of the day trying to work it off. That seemed like a good plan.

One day my temptation finally overwhelmed me. I woke up at my usual six a.m. and walked down to the bakery. It opened at six-thirty, so I was there as they pulled the first tray of Bismarcks out of the oven. I hated being in there surrounded by scones and muffins and cookies. I remember my mother bringing me here as a child and as soon as you walked in the girl behind the counter would give you a cookie. I'm glad they don't do that to adults. What I'm contemplating doing with that Bismarck will be quite enough calories, thank you. I approached the counter half wishing I could turn around and bolt out the door, and half wishing I could just shove every cake, cookie, and loaf of bread in my mouth. I asked the girl behind the counter for a Bismarck and a cup of coffee.

"Can I have the smallest one you have please?" I asked.

"The smallest coffee?" She asked

"No, the smallest Bismarck," I corrected her.

"Oh, Ok..." she said in an annoyed tone and turned to fish out the smallest one. It seemed like it took her an hour and a half to pour my coffee. I threw the money on the counter, which I had already counted out while she was pouring, ignored the little plastic tip cup on the counter since she gave me attitude about getting the smallest Bismarck, and headed straight to a park bench around the corner to eat my feast. I sat down and ripped open the white paper bag. It was already starting to get slightly stained from the butter that was undoubtedly baked into each bite of this bun. Eating one of these would mean at least an hour long run on the beach, but it was worth it. As the first bit of sugar touched my lips, I could sense my stomach jumping. It was as if it couldn't wait for the first bite to enter and it was eager for its arrival. I hadn't eaten anything since yesterday morning, so I guess I didn't have to feel too guilty, but I still did. I wanted to eat it slowly and deliberately, but instead devoured it and licked every bit of cinnamon off my fingers.

A deep feeling of guilt overcame me for what I had just done, as well as depression that I threw my weight loss regime back so far for just a few moments of pleasure. I didn't have such a far walk home but took a long route by the ocean. It gave me time to think about things and start working off that pastry. Growing up at the Jersey Shore I had spent a great deal of time near the water. I loved the beach and loved the whole feel of being near the ocean. I loved it especially when it was the very early morning hours and there was no one on the beach except for a stray runner or dog walker.

Brigantine Island is right over the bridge from Atlantic City. It is much cleaner and prettier. I have slowly watched Atlantic City get more and more grimy from the inside out. Some cities are grimy only on the surface, but Atlantic City is grimy through and through. There is just a sadness that hangs in the air when I drive down the streets of what was once a fun, family-oriented resort town and now see the broken people living on the corner of Greed and Avarice. It depresses me, so I try to stay away from AC. I'm not a gambler and am not enticed into the casinos. On occasion there might be a show that I want to see at one of the hotels, but that is rare. For the most part all I need is on Brigantine and if it isn't there, I can find it off the White Horse Pike in the opposite direction form AC.

I live with my mom in the house that I grew up in. I suppose that isn't very PC these days especially since I am over thirty and unmarried, but I'm comfortable there. I moved back in with my mom after my dad passed away. They were so close; it really devastated her and devastated me to watch her go through so much pain. When I really think about it, the fact that I am thirty and not married does bother me. My dream was to have children, but I just haven't found a man capable of not breaking my heart. I have dated so many men who seemed like Prince Charming in the beginning of the relationship, and by the end of the relationship prove themselves to be far less than charming. I do believe in fairy tales, and dream of being rescued by my knight in shining armor, but I just don't know if I am Princess material.

I know I'm overweight. I'm 5'5" and usually weigh around 110 pounds. My weight tends to go up and down quite a bit. I once ballooned up to 120 lbs. while dating this guy Daryl, who was a chef at The Sands. He would take me to all these great restaurants and make me fabulous meals at home. I was so happy with him; I scarcely noticed the weight gain. I guess he did, because he dumped me for some skinny little thing…at least I assumed she must be skinnier than me. It was such a shock to me since he showed me every day how much he loved me and would do anything for me, and he really did treat me well while we were together. I had no indication that he was unhappy with me. The only thing different about me at the end of the relationship from the beginning of the relationship was that I had those ten extra pounds on me. I never knew it bothered him, in fact he always told me I was too skinny and I needed to put some meat on my bones, I guess once I did, he didn't like the way the 'meat' looked.

The shock of his confession that he didn't love me anymore sent me into a deep deep depression. I felt a lump well up in my throat that made it impossible for me to swallow, therefore, I could not eat. I existed on coffee and an occasional dry bagel. Sometimes I would go a whole day on just half a bagel taking nibbles of it all day long and washing it down with cups and cups of coffee. My hands shook constantly. I would get pepped up for a few minutes from the caffeine, but then I would crash down again, hard, and feel as though I could sleep for days. I worked in a library and would find myself dozing at my desk several times a day. The reverse effect occurred at night, and I hardly slept, I would be constantly exhausted and shaky. I finally got to the point where I could manage to eat a bit more than a bagel, but found I was actually enjoying the smaller sizes I was fitting into, and liked having everyone tell me how much they envied me because I was so thin. Envied me...me! The red-headed, ugly duckling, overweight, lackluster librarian. No one had ever envied me for anything. I guess I finally found something I was good at.

I was feeling weak and tired most of the time, but I also had incredible bursts of energy that were short lived, but very powerful. During those bursts I felt great, I felt so light it was almost as if I were flying. I loved sitting and not feeling a blob of fat falling over my belt. I loved standing and not having to worry that someone was going to stick a sign on me saying 'wide load coming through'. I loved being able to go into a fitting room with the old size fours I used to buy and have them swim on me and have the size zeroes be just right. In fact, shopping became my obsession. I would head to the mall every chance I got and just grab armfuls of size zero clothes to try on. It didn't matter to me that I couldn't afford to buy them all. It just felt so great knowing that if I had the money, I could wear these things and look like the Supermodels do in them.

I couldn't spend too much time in the mall because eventually, it would overwhelm me. I would get extremely tired and I would have to sit down for a while. The only place to sit was the food court, and I couldn't stand to be there with the delectable smells of food swirling around me. It would make me sick to my stomach. Even if I were to give in and have something to eat, everything was in huge portions. I could never eat a whole slice of pizza or a whole burger. Why can't they just sell strawberries individually, or bourbon chicken by the pound so I could get as little as I want instead of having to order this huge serving of it?

If I couldn't take it anymore, I would get coffee and one of those soft, hand rolled pretzels- no salt, and no butter. I would eat half and then accidentally on purpose drop it on the floor and step on it, so I wouldn't be tempted to eat any more of it. After my half pretzel lunch I would have to go home because I would be too bloated to try on any more clothes, and if I did, I would be really depressed because the size zeroes would be too tight.

This was my existence, working in the library all week and Saturdays at the mall. Sundays I would either go to the beach or back to the mall if it were rainy. I loved going to the beach now while there were people there. Before, I was afraid to go when there were others there because I did not want to be seen in a bathing suit. Now I can finally go out in public in a bathing suit, but I still wear a one piece. I am too fat for a two-piece; I would look ridiculous. It is okay to try on dresses and stuff when you're my size, but a bikini is a whole different ball game. You must have a perfect body to wear one of those. There is just no place to hide. I would have to lose a lot more weight before I could wear a bikini. After eating that Bismarck, I may have to wait until next summer.

Lucy Chapter 9

Billy and I set the date. It was a year away and that would give us time to save up some money and get all the arrangements done. My mom kept telling me I was too young, I needed to finish school first, but I was so happy I didn't listen. We booked the local country club, and the plans were underway.

Billy knew what a fan I was of Thoreau so while I oversaw the wedding plans, he booked the honeymoon. We went up to Concord, Massachusetts and visited Walden Pond. It was such a beautiful place to begin our life together. We stayed at the Colonial Inn, which was a big splurge, but well worth it. Our wedding night was all I had hoped it would be and having saved myself for Billy made it even more special. Being in this perfect setting with the man I would love forever was like a dream come true. We walked in the woods by the pond hand in hand and just drank in the serenity and natural calm of this magnificent vista. It was easy to understand why so many great writers, Thoreau, Emerson, and Louisa May Alcott all made Concord their home. I felt inspired to start writing my book while I was up there. I felt like a seed was planted in me that would grow into something beautiful and life changing. I later found out that indeed a seed had been implanted in me at Concord.

Rico Chapter 10

I didn't always ride with the club. Sometimes I just wanted to be on my own. I would take a book and ride to the ocean after work some nights and just find some rock to sit on and read. I have to say I would get some strange looks from people passing me by especially since I had adopted the Mohawk haircut, had a full goatee, had acquired a few tattoos, and pierced an unusual body part or two. Most people don't expect that someone like me reads or even knows how to read, and when they see what I am reading, they usually do a double take. I like 17th century poetry or classics like Dickens, Melville, or Thoreau. My favorite is definitely Thoreau. What I like about him is he was a loner who sort of didn't fit in with society either. He marched to the beat of his own drum. I like when he said,

"If a man does not keep pace with his companions, perhaps it is because he hears a different drummer. Let him step to the music which he hears however measured or far away."

I kind of feel that way too. I put on this tough guy image when I'm with the club, and sometimes even dumb it down, because it's easier not to show you're smart. Once people know you have a brain, they constantly want you to use it for them, not for yourself. They are always asking you questions about shit you don't really care about, and they get pissed if you blow them off, or don't know the answer. That's why I like to live my simple life and not brag about how smart I might be. I do my own thing and fit in when I want to fit in and listen to my own drummer when I want to be alone.

Thoreau was like that too. He wrote about this experiment he did. He leaves town for two years and builds this little cabin in the woods by Walden Pond. True, he wasn't all that far from town, and people could come by and visit him, but while he was there, he lived a simple life. He grew his own food, and mostly read and wrote. I guess if they had Harleys back then he would have jumped on the back of one and headed further away from the town than he did, but he did the best he could for

50

the time he lived in. There was something about the way he described the pond and the peacefulness that made me want to go there.

I often felt pulled to the water. Being a Jersey shore boy, I love the ocean especially the beach at Asbury or Long Beach Island or Brigantine, but any pond or lake was interesting to me. There's just something about bodies of water that calm me down and make me feel reborn. I'd usually ride the bike up as close to the water as I could and just look out over the calm blue and think about all the stuff going on under the water. There was a whole nother world under there that most people don't think about. I remember reading once that we have spent more time exploring the moon than the bottom of the ocean. That's crazy. It's right here! Don't you think some genius would say let's see what we've got, rather than let's go all the way to the moon and see what's there? Things like that make me wonder.

Diana Chapter 11

Sometimes I would notice women on the beach look at me and I knew they were envying how thin I was. I loved it when I could look at a whole beach full of people and know I was the thinnest one there. I was never the 'est' anything. I was never the smartest, prettiest, happiest… never. This was the only thing I could do better than anyone else at least anyone else on this particular beach in New Jersey.

I was at the local grocery store one day in the produce aisle when who should I see there but Daryl! He was with *her*. Seeing her for the first time was shocking! She was actually fatter than I was back when I was at my fattest. I could barely believe it! How could he go for a woman who was bigger than me? I thought the reason he left me was because *I* was fat, and he found me unattractive. So how could he be with this woman that was bigger than me? It just made no sense at all.

"Hello, Daryl" I noticed that he was trying to avert his eyes, but I wasn't going to let him get off the hook that easily. He was squirming and I loved it.

"Hello, Diana, this is Marci, " he said nervously.

"Hello Marci." I was as gracious as can be.

"How have you been, Diana?" I could tell by the way he asked that he still missed me. "You lost so much weight have you been ill?"

So, he did notice. I couldn't help a slight self-satisfied smirk from growing across my face. "No, I've never been better!"

"Well, that's good to hear. We better get going. See you," he said hurriedly.

"Okay, nice meeting you, Marci" they scurried out of the produce aisle and I saw him whisper something in her ear before they disappeared into the soda aisle. I made sure I took a different route through the store. I did not need to see them down each aisle looking so happy and lovey-dovey as they did their grocery shopping. I was glad he noticed that I had lost weight. He was probably missing me, and it made him feel bad that he saw me and couldn't really talk to me because she was around. We used to talk all the time. I could tell him about everything. I would tell him about my day at work and my parents and my friends and my former jobs. Everything. He would listen like he really empathized with me. He seldom said much himself. He was the quiet type. He just let me talk and talk and talk. That was one of the things I loved most about him.

I am not sure what went wrong with him and me. I thought we had a great time together. He loved going to all the same places I did. He never complained about anything. He was an easy boyfriend to have. I never really thought much about our relationship. I guess I just took it for granted that he would always be there for me.

I thought we were moving in the direction of marriage. I could only imagine that he left me because I was fat. There could have been no other reason. Now that I see that he left me for an even fatter woman, she had to be at least a size eight, I was totally baffled. I started to feel sickened and I emptied the few things I had put in my cart and left the store. I lost my appetite anyway.

This brief encounter hit me hard. I couldn't stop thinking about Daryl and really couldn't imagine why he left me. I went home where my mom said her usual, "I'm worried about you...you look too skinny." I always just shrugged it off. She had no idea how happy I was with my new body. It was the only thing in my life that I seemed to be getting right. It was easy. If I watched what I ate, I could keep losing weight and get the body

I always wanted and needed.

The best thing about working in a library is you get to read on the job, and nobody stops you or questions you. I love to read. I would gravitate towards classic literature. I loved Louisa May Alcott and Thoreau. Alcott was a very strong independent woman who spoke her mind and didn't apologize to anyone. I truly admired her and wished I could have been more like her. Thoreau and his trip to the woods to live deliberately fascinated me. I wondered what he ate in the woods. I wondered if he lost weight while he was there? I bet that would be a good way to take off some pounds. He ate a mostly vegetarian diet and ate a lot of wild fruit and vegetables. It sounded like a good plan. I often thought about why he went to the woods and that quote:

"I went to the woods because I wished to live deliberately, to front only the essential facts of life, and see if I could not learn what it had to teach, and not, when I came to die, discover that I had not lived."

I wondered if I would reach the end of my life and discover I had not lived. That thought terrified me. I wasn't sure what I wanted to do about that terror, but there was something about that quote that insisted I keep it filed away in the back of my mind and look at it every now and then. What does living deliberately mean? Is it doing what you mean to do? Is it living with a sense of purpose or a reason for being? Is it living each moment with an appreciation for your surroundings? I was not sure, but I knew one day I had to go deeper into that very phrase and find what was locked up in it as a lesson I should learn. Right now, I didn't feel as though I was living deliberately or otherwise, nor did I care.

As I walked past the library, I was thinking about this woman I met there. I was working one Thursday when a woman came in and asked me for books on skin cancer and Thoreau. I thought that was an odd combination but being such a big Thoreau fan, I struck up a conversation with her. She said she was also a Thoreau fan and was going to this

Annual Gathering in Concord, Massachusetts the second weekend in July. She started talking about why it was so important to her to go. She said she had just been diagnosed with malignant melanoma and was very scared. She said she always wanted to see Walden Pond and that her favorite Thoreau quote was,

"I went to the woods because I wished to live deliberately, to front only the essential facts of life, and see if I could not learn what it had to teach, and not, when I came to die, discover that I had not lived."

She had to run to pick up her twins from soccer practice, but she would come back tomorrow to chat. She introduced herself as Madeline, and I told her my name was Diana. I spent the rest of the afternoon looking for books that would be of interest to Madeline. I found books on surviving skin cancer, as well was books on Thoreau and by Thoreau. I put them all aside for her to pick up on her visit tomorrow.

She came back the next day as promised and we chatted some more about literature in general, Thoreau in particular. She told me it was not too late to make reservations for the Thoreau weekend if I was interested. She said there would even be room in the car with her and her family if I wanted to drive up with them. I told her I did like the idea, but I had to think about it. It was June and the trip was a month away. I guess I could plan something that far in advance; I just wasn't sure how I would feel in a month.

A weekend in Concord, Mass with a focus on Thoreau and his writings and an opportunity to spend time at Walden Pond. This sounded like heaven and something I very much wanted to do, but the trip was a month away and I just didn't know how I would feel in a month. The encounter with Daryl upset me still. I didn't want to feel too weak to travel, but I didn't want to miss this opportunity either. I was sure it would be good for me, but then, was I looking for something good for me? In the back of my mind I knew that I was getting weaker, but I couldn't stop what I was doing. Maybe I was dying deliberately?

After all these thoughts from the past month swirled through my head, I finally reached home from my bakery excursion and even though I was exhausted, I decided I had to pick up the pace and exercise it off. I dressed in heavy sweats hoping to perspire the bun right out of me since it was a hot day already and went to the beach to jog. This was one of those summer mornings that promise to be a scorcher by midday. It was already quite sunny, and the temperature had to be at least eighty degrees. It was also very humid. I could not have run more than a quarter mile when I remember seeing this guy on a motorcycle not too far from me. I must have passed out. I do not remember a thing. I woke up in the back of an ambulance with some stupid paramedic trying to shove an IV needle in me. Those things are full of calories, there was no way he was going to stick that in me. I was pretty week, but I managed to rip it out of my arm. I heard them say restraints, and then I passed out again.

The next time I woke up I was in the Frank Sinatra wing of the Atlantic City Hospital in a room with an IV pole dangling at my side. I tried to rip it out but soon realized I could not move my arms; I was in shackles. What was going on? This had to be a mistake. Why were they treating me like a criminal? What had I done? I felt like I had been dropped into a nightmare. Was I being punished for eating the Bismarck? A nurse came in and I asked her what happened. She said I was running along the beach and passed out. I was severely dehydrated and malnourished. Malnourished? This is America. How could I be malnourished? I just ate a whole Bismarck for heaven's sake! Okay, I know I have been watching what I eat, but I was certainly not malnourished. Malnourishment implies you have not taken in what your body needs. I was taking in exactly what I needed to take in if I were to succeed at what I hoped to do.

"Miss, do you know your name? You had no identification on you."

My head was pounding so fiercely that every word she said in that obnoxious voice of hers reverberated through my skull. "Diana, my name is Diana." I answered just hoping it would make her stop talking.

"Diana what?"

"Diana Sewell. I live on Brigantine"

Good Diana, we will call your family."

"Why… am I… in shackles?"

"You have been trying to rip out your intravenous. You need to get the nutrients from it. You almost went into a coma."

A coma! How could that be? It must have been the heat. "Can you…take these shackles off me… now?"

"I'll have to check with your doctor."

'Please…I promise I'll leave the IV in," I begged.

"I'll speak to the doctor and get back to you. Do you want to see your friend now?"

"My friend?"

"Yes, the gentleman who found you on the beach."

"Here? I didn't…know how I got here." The nurse went outside for a second and came in with this rather scary looking guy, but he had very kind green/brown eyes. He had a Mohawk haircut, lots of tattoos, was pierced in many places, and wearing a leather vest with nothing under it. I realized he was the biker I saw on the beach.

"Diana, this is Rico. You are very lucky he came along when he did, he saved your life."

I could tell by her introduction that I was supposed to be grateful to this guy. Why did she think I would be happy that he saved my life? Why did he have to butt in where he did not belong? Aren't guys who look like him supposed to kill people, not save them? It was all very confusing, but I figured I should be polite; the guy did go out of his way to come see how I was. "Thank you." I could not really say much more than that, I was still pretty weak.

"You OK, Slim? You gave us all a good scare." He said.

"Too hot...saw you on the beach." I could not muster up the strength to speak coherently.

"Yeah, I was there, then I saw you go down. I started doing CPR, then I called into my gas station to call the ambulance. Thank God for mobile phones, right?"

"Yes...thank God..."

"Look, you get some rest, and I'll check in on you tomorrow. Do me a favor, eat something. You look like you could use a good juicy steak. You ain't gonna get that here in the hospital, but when you get better, I'm buying. Ok?"

"...Thanks..." The librarian in me usually bristles when I hear the word "ain't" but for some reason coming from him it did not bother me. I do not remember if I said anything after that or even what I had heard him

58

say, something about buying me a steak, I think. I could not think about food right now. I just wanted to die. I was so angry this guy pulled me off the beach. Why did he have to get involved? My life is not worth saving. I drifted off to sleep and was awakened by my mom standing over me.

"Diana, what happened?"

"Just passed out mom...was too hot to jog." I was feeling a bit stronger now, because of the IV. They still had me shackled and I was really angry, but too weak to fight. I didn't want to get better; I just wished everyone would leave me alone.

"It's because you don't eat. I knew this would happen. Why are you doing this?'

"I'm not doing anything, Mom, I'm just thin, that's all. Please do not badger me Mom, I have a really bad headache."

"Well you have me heartsick over this. I'm going to make them keep you here until you gain some weight."

"No! You can't do that to me! I'm an adult.... you can't keep me here against my will."

'Diana, you almost died, what will it take for you to wake up?''

Rico Chapter 12

You never know what you're going to find on the beach. Last week I went to this beach near Atlantic City called Brigantine Beach. It's much cleaner than AC and quieter. I parked the bike and was walking along the beach early on this hot muggy morning when there was practically nobody else there. I see this real skinny girl jogging in the hot sun wearing this unbelievably heavy jogging suit and I see she's starting to sway. Before I know it, she's down. The garage I work in's got this poster on how to do CPR and I stare at this thing everyday, so I guess I kind of memorized it. I go running over and check to see if she's breathing, she ain't, so I start doing compressions. She starts breathing and I use my two-way phone to call the garage and tell them to send an ambulance. She was so tiny. First, I thought she was just a kid, but she was just really thin. Once she came to, she was hallucinating a bit. She kept saying "Let me die, I want to die." I felt bad for her. Why would anyone want to die? There are so many cool things to see in this world I want to experience them all. I can't imagine wishing you were dead.

I went by the hospital that day to check on her. Her name was Diana, but I called her Slim to try to make her smile. I brought her some wildflowers because I always liked this quote Thoreau had about wildflowers. She was really weak, and they said she'd been trying to rip out her IV, so they had her restrained. She looked so sad. I just wanted to cheer her up. They said she would have died on the beach if I hadn't been there, but I just did what anyone would do. It really bothered me when she talked about wanting to die. I figured I wouldn't mention it when I talked to her and just keep things light. I tried to give her some things to look forward to. I told her I would come by to see her the next day, and that when she got out I would take her for a steak dinner and that I wanted her to promise me she'd eat and get stronger. My guess was she was anorexic. She was so pathetically thin and was trying to rip out her IV. I knew a girl like that in high school. It was really sad. She eventually ended up killing herself. I always felt bad about doing nothing to help her, but we didn't know each other well, and I only found out about how sick in the head she was after she was already dead. Maybe this time I could do something.

I guess it's true that everybody gets their fifteen minutes of fame, because when I left the hospital there was this camera crew and reporter there asking me questions. My mom said I was on the 6:00 news and there was an article about me saving this woman's life in the Asbury Park Press. I don't like any kind of attention, so I figured I'd hang out in AC for a few more days before going home. My mom's cute. When I got back home, she had this sign up in the dining room welcoming me home, and she said I was a hero, and she was proud of me. I never told them about saving Nicky, little did they know she was the second life I saved. My dad just kept patting me on the back and had this real big grin on his face. That made me feel good. My folks gave up trying to judge me, or make me feel like I should be doing more with my life, but I guess as a kid you always want to please them, so I was glad I could do something that made them proud, and maybe gave them something they could brag to their friends about. I never tried to do nothing just to impress people, but if I could make my folks proud of me, that was like a bonus.

This Diana situation made me start thinking about life and death. It was something my mind would occasionally slip to, but it's not like I get all nuts about it. I was just thinking about my life and the things I want to do. I've been feeling the need for a change. The easy thing to do when you feel that way is change the way you look. That's a no brainer. You can always get a new tattoo, cut your hair, grow your hair, dye your hair, but it's changing what's under your hair that's hard. I feel sometimes like I want to change my head, or at least put some different stuff in there. I don't see myself being a mechanic all my life. It was great as a kid to be able to spend all day working on engines and bikes and know something like a machine was never going to keep me from going somewhere because if it broke down, I could fix it. Wheels will never be a problem for me. As long as there's a road that leads to it, I can get there. But where am I going? I'm hitting thirty this year and I've been thinking a lot about the future. The day I bought the bike from Richie, I know was a terrible day for him, but he did it for his wife. I remember thinking how whipped this guy must be to let some woman control him like that. Then I find out from Nicky that she wanted him to stop riding because he was dying, and she wanted to spend as much time as possible with him before he was gone. Even though I've never had that kind of love in my life, I know Lucy has that and I've been thinking it might be nice.

Lucy Chapter 13

Things really started out great with us. We were so young and in love and just excited to be near each other. It was a great time.

I remember what it felt like to be a newlywed. I started the semester with a new name and a new piece of jewelry. I wore my wedding ring proudly and was the envy of all the other girls because I was lucky enough to get a guy like Billy. He was the Captain of the baseball team and in the time we were dating had really come out of his shell. He said he spent his childhood living in an overweight body and kids teased him mercilessly. It left him insecure and shy especially around girls, but also driven to achieve, to prove all his tormentors wrong when they chanted that he was a loser. He always said it was me who brought out the best in him.

The first week of school was a bit of an adjustment. We had moved into the basement apartment in my mother and father's house. We could not afford anything else, but it was fine. We were just happy to be together.

Billy studied pre-law and dreamed of going to law school. I was studying English with a focus on Journalism. I still dreamed of writing the great American novel.

Billy was working two jobs so we could start saving money towards a place of our own, and we would also need to have something in the bank to float us while he was in law school. I was working a job after school in a chocolate shop on the boardwalk in Asbury Park. We tried to spend every free moment together, but we had a great deal of family obligations and we tried to please everyone. Sometimes during times of stress my period tends to be a little late so I didn't even give it a second thought, but when over two months went by and Big Red hadn't come to town yet, I got a home pregnancy test. Low and behold, I was pregnant! The doctor confirmed I was ten weeks along, which meant I had gotten pregnant on our honeymoon in Concord.

That afternoon seemed so long while I waited in our little love nest for Billy to come home from class. I could not wait to give him the news. We had never really discussed when we would start a family, but I knew he wanted kids and I knew he would be a great father. My mom was home that afternoon, but I had to contain myself from running upstairs to share the good news with her. Billy had to know first. This was in the pre-cell phone and pager days, so I couldn't get in touch with him while he was at school or commuting. The suspense grew. Rico was away on one of his biker weekends, and I was glad for that because if he had been around, I knew I couldn't keep the good news from him. It was getting close to three o'clock and I knew Mom would be asking me to come up for coffee soon. We had this little ritual where I would go upstairs around three o'clock and have coffee with my mom while she got dinner ready and tell her about my day. I couldn't go up today because I knew I wouldn't be able to keep this secret from her. I went to the bottom of the stairs and called up "Mom, I have a lot of homework, I'm going to skip coffee today."

"Oh, ok, Lucy" was the reply. I could tell she was disappointed. I hated lying to her, but I just couldn't let her know before Billy.

As the time approached for him to return home my anxiety grew. His class ended at 3:45. By the time he stopped at his locker, and walked to his car, it was usually 4:30 when he got home. He always brought a note he wrote me, or a flower he picked, or just a big kiss, but he never came home without something special for me. This afternoon was no different. He came through the door at 4:32, gave me a huge hug and kiss and slipped a little note in my hand. It simply said, "I missed you today and I can't wait to spend the rest of the evening with you. Let's skip dinner with mom and dad tonight, I want you all to myself…Love, Billy."

I read the note and was at once relieved, because although I love my folks, I wanted to spend this night with just Billy after I told him the news. Then it hit me. He wanted me all to himself? He would never have me all to himself again. He would be sharing me with our child and there would be precious little alone time from now on. I had not been thinking about it from that angle and now I was scared. I assumed he would be as happy as I was, but what if he wasn't? I decided I could not think like that. Of course, he would be thrilled. A new little life was created that was part him, part me and born out of our immense love for each other. Even though we had not been married for very long, we were totally in love and knew we eventually would start a family. Maybe not five minutes into our marriage, but some day.

I could barely stand the anticipation any longer, I had to tell him. I took his hand and led him to the fold-out couch. He started kissing me and taking my blouse off. I resisted a bit and said, "I have something important to tell you first."

"Okay, shoot, just make it quick because I want to make love to you right now!"

"I went to the doctor today." Suddenly, his little boy excitement at the thought of having me was replaced with concern. His face got serious and he sat straight up.

"Are you okay, you didn't tell me you weren't feeling well, what's wrong?"

"I'm fine, I was just concerned because my period was so late."

"But you said that happens to you sometimes when you are stressed"

"Yes, it does, but I just wanted to get it checked out and the doctor gave me some wonderful news!"

"You're okay?"

"I'm better than okay, I'm pregnant!" When the words left me lips, I was extremely happy until I saw his face and felt him pull his body away. It was such a noticeable retreat, that it felt as though he was no longer even in the same room as me, and a cold rush of air was now between us. He sat there silently for what seemed like a month, then he got up. I was stunned. That certainly was not the reaction I had dreamed of. I said "Aren't you happy? Aren't you going to say anything?"

"I thought you were taking the pill?" Was all he could muster.

"I was, but the doctor said since I was on antibiotic for a sinus infection it could have made the pill ineffective."

It all happened so fast. One minute I was elated, the next minute my whole world fell apart. He got so mad and picked up the Lenox vase my Aunt Rita had given us for my shower. He was about to smash it when I grabbed it from him. He called me a stupid bitch and smacked me so hard across the face that I landed on the fold-out. I screamed at him to get out and leave me alone. My lip was bleeding. I must have bitten it when I fell. The blood scared him, and he left. I half expected my mom or dad to come to the door asking what happened. They surely could hear the shouting since their bedroom was right above our couch, but they chose to ignore it. Looking back, now that I am a parent I can't possibly understand how parents can hear their daughter getting hit and not run to help her, but I learned a lot of nasty things about my parents, particularly my mother, that day and they were tough lessons to learn. I needed Rico more than ever and wished some of his friends were around. I decided I could never tell Rico about this because he would kill Billy for hurting me. I just collapsed on the fold-out and started to cry. I could feel the baby was as sad as I was with the events of the day.

The new hormones racing through my body started to kick into overdrive and I just continued to cry. Mom must have been looking out the window and saw Billy leave which was unusual since when he came home, she knew she wouldn't hear from us for at least an hour while we got to know each other again. I guess she did hear me crying but didn't want to get involved while Billy was still home. In no time I heard a knock on my door. She wanted to know if everything was all right and if she could come down. I really did not know what I would say to her, but I needed someone to hug me and tell me everything would be all right. I really needed my mom. She came down with coffee for each of us and the excuse that she thought I might need a cup since I was studying so hard.

Of course, she noticed the tears. She sat down on the fold-out next to me in the very spot where Billy had just been and asked what was wrong. I told her I was pregnant, and Billy had a really bad reaction to it.

Mom had very old-fashioned ideas and often her concept of what the world should be like directly contradicted mine. I thought this news would shock her, but nothing in my wildest dreams could have prepared me for the reaction I got. "Of course he's upset, what's wrong with you? You're only twenty years old and still in college. You've only been married for two and a half months and can't even support yourselves, now you want to support a baby too? What were you thinking? How are you going to live with Billy starting law school and another mouth to feed?"

What she said next totally blew me away. We were raised Catholic and I thought my parent's morals coincided with mine, but when the next sentence came out of my mother's mouth, my world and all I thought I knew about it and its inhabitants turned upside-down. "You have to have an abortion."

I felt like I had been dropped into a foreign release of an American movie where you recognize the actors, but you can't understand a word they are saying and I couldn't see the subtitles either.

"WHAT???? You cannot be serious? I couldn't live with myself. Do you realize what you are asking me to do?" I knew I could never look at myself in the mirror again or see a baby and not wonder about the one I killed. "How can you ask me to do this?"

"You're getting dramatic Lucy."

"Dramatic? You just asked me to do something horrible and you expect me not to react? This is my life and my baby's life. You think I can do something that dreadful that will alter it forever?"

"You're pregnant, Lucy, you already did something that will alter your life forever."

"But the outcome will be a good thing, a new life, my child, your grandchild. In your plan I will have nothing but guilt and shame and nightmares. How could you ask me to do that?"

"Lucy, you just don't understand how difficult it is to bring a child into this world when you are in this situation."

"What are you talking about, you were about my age when you got pregnant with Rico and you and Dad managed." As the words left my mouth, I realized what she was trying to say. She wished she had aborted Rico and did not have to struggle with being a young mother. The thought of it physically sickened me and I had to run to the bathroom for my first pregnancy vomit. From the bathroom I called out to her to go, and leave me alone, I didn't want to talk to her anymore.

I heard her footsteps going up the stairs and as I hung over the toilet the reality hit me that I lost my mother and husband in the span of about 10 minutes. My brother's life and probably mine too had been an inconvenience to my mother. I started to piece things together and realized that I never saw a wedding picture of my parents and she was always very hedgy about when their anniversary was. She also talked all the time about the fact that she gave up going to Dental school to have children. Until that moment I never realized how much she hated the fact that we messed up her plans and put her life on a different track. It could have been out of love for me that she did not want to see me doing the same thing she did, but this was a different situation. I was married, I did not have a career in the works yet, and I really want this baby. All I had in this world was this baby and I would fight to the death to protect it. I couldn't understand why the rest of my world was not as happy as I was.

I am not stupid. I knew it was going to be a struggle, but I just couldn't do what my mother was suggesting. No matter what her motivation was for suggesting it, I could not forgive her for wanting to put me through the heartache of killing my own child. I also could not forgive her for resenting me and my brother all this time. I really wished Rico had been home. He was the only one I thought could have made some sense out of all this for me. Then it hit me that he may not know he was the reason for our parent's hasty marriage. I did not want to be the one to tell him and make him feel the incredible resentment I was now feeling from my mother. I could never imagine resenting this baby. We bonded a lot that day, my baby and me, and together we would conquer any adversity.

This day had just been too much for me and I needed to rest. Thankfully, tomorrow I had an early class so I would throw myself into my schoolwork and not think of these past events. It would be hard, but I had to. I needed to come up with a plan for how I was going to get through this next year of school and raise this baby. This year would be okay since I was due in May and would be done with school by then. It was next year that I had to worry about. The semester had just started so maybe I could take an extra course this semester and an extra one next semester and that would mean two less courses next year. I drifted off to sleep thinking of all the things I needed to do tomorrow.

I must have been asleep for about twenty minutes when I felt someone shaking me. It was Billy. He had come back with a big bouquet of flowers from Wawa. "Lucy, I am so sorry. I never should have treated you like that. I was just shocked by the news. You are right. We will get through this. I promise I will be there for you and our baby."

I was so happy to hear him say that. I pulled him close to me and hugged him tightly. I loved Billy so much and I knew he loved me. He only hit me because he was confused. He is usually the sweetest guy in the world. Everything was going to be all right. Billy and I would make this work. We could get through any obstacles we had to face. My mother, that would be another story. I fell back to sleep in his arms and felt confident that tomorrow would be a better day.

Well, tomorrow was a better day. Billy told his parents who had a much better reaction than my mom did, but their disappointment was not unnoticeable. We talked extensively with both sets of parents to figure out what our next step would be. My parents agreed to let us stay in the basement for a very minimal rent and my in-laws would help us get someone to watch the baby while I finished school. They also said they would give us a loan to help when Billy went to law school so there would not be the added pressure on him to work full time. Things seemed to be falling into place. There was still a tremendous air of negativity and it hurt me to think that at what should be the happiest time of my life, no one was happy for me. I understand that this was an inconvenient time to be pregnant, but couldn't everyone just try to act as though this was a wonderful thing instead of a tragedy? I could only hope that as time wore on everyone would accept this. The only one truly happy for me was Rico. I swear if he could knit, he'd be making some little leather baby booties.

A few weeks later the family got some great news. Aunt Kris was pregnant! We were all so delighted for her. My mom was her older sister and quickly started preparing a baby shower. She was due right around the time I was, and it would be so nice to have our babies grow up together. I always thought of her as more like an older sister than an Aunt. She is exactly ten years younger than my mom and ten years older than me, so she bridges the generation gap between the two of us. I was sure that this shower was going to be a joint shower for the two of us and I was so impressed with mom's ability to keep that a secret from me. She had me make all the favors since I had a flair for making chocolate. How clever of mom to include me in the plans! When the day of the shower came, I told myself I would act surprised even though I knew exactly what was going on.

The shower was at Aunt Meg's house. I went with mom, and Aunt Kris would be arriving under the impression that it was a birthday party for my niece Karly. I figured Mom would spring the surprise on me after Aunt Kris walked in and I spent the whole afternoon in anticipation until the party was almost over and all the presents were opened, and the cake came rolling out that said 'Congratulations Kris'. That really hurt. I said to my mom, "I thought this was going to be a shower for both of us."

"You don't deserve a shower. Kris has been married for years and has been trying so hard to have a baby. You should not even be pregnant, and you think you deserve a shower? I am still not happy about this." She snapped in reply.

This really hurt. I took mom's silence these past few months as acceptance. Nothing could have been further from the truth. As I got bigger and bigger so did her resentment of the situation and of me. She was getting more and more uncomfortable with each pound I gained. She would never accept the situation or accept me, or my baby. I had to realize that was a fact and try to live my life the best way I could.

I spent a lot of time praying over this. This very kind priest, Father Joe, told me everything would be okay. He said I had taken the good path by choosing to have my baby and not have an abortion. He said remember, Mary had a hard time because of what was deemed an inconvenient pregnancy but look how that turned out! That made me feel better. I felt as though I made the right decision and even if everyone was not thrilled with my choice, it was my choice and it was the right choice.

I endured six more months of my mother and Billy's verbal abuse and Billy's occasional physical abuse. My mother never let an opportunity go by to tell me how disappointed she was in me. We were really struggling financially and would have been on the streets if my parents did not let us live with them, and they reminded us of this all the time. I was out of school, but unable to find any kind of job that would pay enough for me to pay a sitter. My mom was barely speaking to me, and my mother and father in-law had retired to Florida.

Rico has no idea what's going on in my marriage. Billy is intimidated by him, so he never raises his voice and certainly not his hands to me around Rico. I know if I ever told Rico that Billy hits me, Rico and his friends would 'take care' of him. As much as I hate him a times, he still is my husband and in the back of my mind I feel that maybe the old Billy I used to love will come back and mean Billy will go away.

Billy Chapter 14

Lucy and I married our junior year. I needed someone in my life to balance out the two sides of my personality, and besides, she wouldn't sleep with me until we were married so I was in a hurry to run down that aisle. I wanted to do anything in my power to make Lucy happy, so I booked our honeymoon in the place that she talked about all the time, Concord, Massachusetts. Being from Boston, Concord was my backyard, and I did not find it particularly exciting, but she always talked about it and wanted to go there. When she spoke about Concord, she radiated a glow which seemed to engulf me. I wanted to give her this as my wedding gift, one which I would receive great benefit from as well because making her happy made me happy. She talked as though this was a mission. She didn't just want to go to Concord she *needed* to go. Most women would beg to go to Hawaii or Europe, my Lucy just wanted to go to Concord, Massachusetts. How could I say no?

Life could not have been better. We were both in school, looking forward to a future with each other, living in my in-law's basement apartment, and having sex all the time. We didn't have many expenses and my part-time job covered most of it. I also had a tiny inheritance from Granny which was going to go towards law school.

I loved Lucy so much. I could not have been happier. Then I had another of those best-and-worst all rolled into one days. Lucy told me she was pregnant. We had only been married a few months, we barely had any alone time and now we were going to be a family. I immediately started worrying that this would alter my plans to go to law school and force me to take some menial job to support my family. I was so angry, that I did not even focus on the fact that my beautiful Lucy was about to give me a child. I could only think of myself and how this was going to inconvenience me. I did the only thing I knew how to do. I yelled, I cursed at her, and I hit her. I had never laid a hand on her before. I was horrified at myself but took the anger out on her somehow convincing myself that it was her fault, and my response was justifiable.

I left the apartment and went to a bar. I got drunk, picked up a girl whose name I never even asked, and had sex with her in the backseat of the car that would soon contain a baby car seat. After I climaxed it was as if the anger left my body and I realized what I had done. I felt horrible. My head was pounding, and I felt like the worst kind of loser. What had I done to Lucy? How could I be so stupid? I drove the girl home and stopped at an all-night Wawa to get some flowers for Lucy, went home and begged her to forgive me. She had a welt on her face where I smacked her, and she knew I had been drinking, but I don't think she suspected I had cheated on her. She forgave me and I felt a bit jealous that she should be able to forgive me when I could not forgive myself. Why did she have to be so much better than me?

Rico Chapter 15

There's something about the thought of having a kid that I could play ball with or go for walks on the beach with picking up shells or just teach them to love life that appeals to me, and has been creeping into my mind a lot lately. Of course, before the kids, there'd have to be a woman, and the women I've been attracting lately are not really what you'd call wife and mother material. Oh well, for now, I like being on my own. If it happens one day, I'll probably like that too.

Until that day happens, I still have a lot of adventures ahead of me. That book Walden got me psyched to go see the Pond. I had some vacation time coming to me from the garages, so I decided I would get a map and hop on the bike and ride up to Concord, Massachusetts where Walden Pond is. It was the second week in July, and it was way hot, but as you're riding you have this nice cool breeze thing going on, and it can actually get pretty chilly at night. I did the I-95 route for a while, but sometimes got off and took Route 1. It's got a lot of lights, but you really don't see the country from '95. Especially driving through New England. Every town you drive through looks the same. Stamford, Bridgeport, New Haven, same, same, same. I like to see new things. I rode my hog from 95 to 91 to 84 to the Mass Pike, then into Concord. I would occasionally pass a biker while in Connecticut without a helmet on. Man, that's just plain whack. I know they don't have to ride with helmets up here, but you gotta be all kinds of shades of stupid to not wear one. If you drop your bike, your head is going to hit the pavement first. Why would anyone take that kind of chance?

I got into Concord Friday morning. I like riding early in the morning. It's peaceful, except for the sound of my own engines. I like the way the sky looks before the cars are out, and I like the way the air feels. It feels different in the morning and makes me feel different. Sort of like a coolness with a little mist still in it. It reminds me of the way the air feels all day long at the beach. It's sort of like the air really wants to be beach air, and gets its wish in the early morning hours, but then for the rest of the day it must be regular air.

There was something even more special about the air once I got to route 2-West in Mass. It was cleaner, somehow lighter, and a little different. I wanted to see Walden Pond, and that was my only plan. I didn't know how long I would stay in Mass, or what I would find once I got there. I just knew that it was where I needed to be right now. I followed the signs to Walden Pond. There was this little gift shop nearby with a ton of books by my man Henry. I picked up this new one <u>Wild Fruits</u> Now the guy's been dead for almost 150 years so how is it possible that there is a new book by him on the shelves? I ask the guy in the store and I found out it was a just released manuscript that's been edited and is now on the shelves. Pretty cool I thought, so I plunked down my $17.95, put it in my backpack and I was out of there.

My next stop was the Pond. It was so beautiful. I was glad I chose to park my hog far away and walk, because I really didn't want to disturb the peacefulness of this place. This ain't Jersey. The sky's so clear, there's a crispness that just fills the whole place. Sometimes I feel like I don't belong places. I get some weird stares when I walk into a bank or the post office because of my hair and the way I dress, but I don't give a crap. They're only seeing the outside of me, and I know that I am not your average biker. Then sometimes when I say something intelligent I get strange looks from the bikers, and I couldn't care less about that either, because I know who I am, and I may be different and not quite fit in with either world, but I like my world and I don't hurt nobody by being me. I'd only been here a few hours, but I felt like I totally fit in. I felt like I could be close to nature and read without anybody even thinking twice, and nobody was judging me because of the way I was dressed. I hadn't gotten a single funny stare yet. This wasn't no fashion show. It was just people with something in common sharing the air of this special place, and then moving on with their lives. I really liked it here.

It was getting kind of late and I was getting pretty hungry, so I decided to head into Concord to grab something to eat and find a place to stay. I tried about six places and they were all booked. It seems there was this gathering of this Thoreau Society going on this weekend and all the rooms in town were taken. I get to this place, the Colonial Inn and they have one room left, but they say they have to give it to two people because it's a suite, and there are just no other rooms available in town. The clerk at the desk asks if I will share the room with this yuppie-looking guy who's standing at the other end of the counter. Hey, I have no problem, I just want to crash, but this guy looks like he's going to have a heart attack when they ask him if he'll share the room with me. I could tell he was looking for a good reason to say no, but I guess he was as tired as I was, because he said he'd take the room.

So, we get up to the suite, it was nice we each had our own bedroom, but had to share a bathroom and common area. We made our intros, his name was Jason, and I guess he looked relieved that I don't bite. I went to my room and just plopped down on the bed for a few minutes, but I didn't want to get too comfortable, because I really needed a shower, so I got back up again. The guy was in the bathroom, so I took my new book and go out to the terrace that was off the common area to wait. He came out a few minutes later and seemed surprised that I'm reading Wild Fruits. I'm not sure he was surprised I'm reading Thoreau or that I can read at all. Turns out he's reading Wild Fruits too. It also turns out he's from the town right next to mine in Jersey.

He grew up in West Long Branch. This guy's got bucks, but I start talking to him and I found out he's a bit of a rebel himself. He never quite fit in with the rich kids he hung with, because he was a bit of a free spirit and wanted to do his own thing. He dresses the part of Mr. Corporate America, but his heart is in the woods being close to nature and reading like me.

His mom was a school principal, and his dad was a developer who built malls. He has a brother Doug. Both his mom and dad weren't around much. He said he was practically raised by his nanny. I kind of felt bad for him. Even though my folks had to work a lot, they always made sure they spent as much time with us as they could and if there was something important going on in one of our lives, they were there for us. He said he and his brother were great tennis players, but his folks never were able to make it to one match. One thing I like about leading a simple life is I don't have to worry about pissing off the wrong people or climbing any corporate ladder. If I want to get up and go, I get up and go. If my boss don't like it, I can find a job someplace else. There's thousands of gas stations in Jersey. Damn sure if I had a kid, and my kid had something important going on at school, I would be there.

He tells me this story about the job he was just fired from. He went to Princeton and his dad pushed him into finance even though he would have preferred something more in the field of science or environmentalism. He gets this job with this investment banking company and this hotshot Nicholas Rockford takes him under his wing. This Rockford guy is about to start managing his own fund, which is a real big deal I gather in the finance world. Rockford makes a bonehead mistake that Jason tried to talk him out of, but instead of saying 'I told you so', Jason takes the heat for Rockford and tells all the big wigs that he gave Nicholas faulty data. He saved this guy's corporate ass and got fired. "So, what made you come up here?" I asked.

"Well, here I was almost thirty, out of work, a decent amount of money in the bank, but no clue as to what I would do with my life. I decided I needed to clear my head. I needed to take a trip somewhere peaceful, calm and quiet, where I could have some quiet reflection on my life and what I should do next. I always wanted to see Walden Pond and

Concord. Thoreau's book <u>Walden</u> was always an inspiration to me. This seemed like a good place to start to find myself. I found out there was going to be this Annual Gathering of the Thoreau Society, so I signed up. Unfortunately, it was too late for me to get a room in the Concord Academy, so I just thought I 'd take my chances and see if I could get another room up here."

He said this guy Rockford was really grateful and promised to set him up in whatever kind of business he wanted, so Jason came here to try to figure out what he wants to do with his life. His story reminded me of the way I saved Nicky from those other bikers. The corporate world and the street world ain't all that different. We talked a lot and the more we talked, the more we found out we had a lot in common. He even had heard of me saving that girl on the beach. He said he always wanted to play football, but his folks made him play tennis, because they thought football was too dangerous. He went to some expensive private school that didn't offer football anyway.

It's kind of weird; we both became Thoreau fans after we read the same quote. It goes:

"If a man does not keep pace with his companions, perhaps it is because he hears a different drummer. Let him step to the music which he hears however measured or far away."

It described the two of us perfectly. Neither of us quite kept pace with the dudes we hung out with, we both sort of heard our own music, and that was okay.

Jason had this whole list of things to do with the Thoreau people and he asked me if I was interested in doing any of it. That afternoon there was going to be this dude dressed up like Thoreau reading <u>Life Without Principal</u> on the steps of the First Parish Church. That sounded cool so I went with him to that. I love that essay. It's where Thoreau really sticks it to the politicians. After it was over, we got up to go and I see this woman with curly, long red hair coming towards me.

"Rico!"

"Slim!" I was so surprised to see her here. I said "Hey, you look great, baby!" She gives me this big hug. It was so nice to get a hug. There still ain't much meat on her bones, but she felt good wrapped around me.

"What a surprise to see you here" She echoed my thoughts. "I'm really glad too since I never really got to thank you for saving my life."

"Hey, I'm just glad you're better and you're here. You didn't look so good the last time I saw you, but you're lookin' good now!"

"I've been doing a lot of thinking, and I've been eating like you told me to. I have a good friend who helped me put things in perspective." She then introduced me to the woman standing next to her. "This is my friend Madeline, and these are her twins Mark and Matthew."

I extended my hand to each of the boys and Madeline. Madeline had this scarf around her head, and I could only see peach fuzzy hair under the scarf. My guess was that she was a cancer patient, and that having a friend facing death with no choice about it must have been what put things in perspective for Slim. I introduced them all to Jason. We found out we were all from Jersey. We talked for a bit and then Madeline and her family left. Jason excused himself since he was tired. That left me and Slim. "So, how bout that steak dinner?" I asked.

"You mean here? In Concord?"

"Yeah, why not? There's this really nice place down the road, the

Colonial Inn." I didn't want to tell her that was where I was staying in case she thought I had other ideas. "I hear they have really good food. What do you say?"

"Sure. I'd like that! But I should be treating you…after all, I wouldn't be here if you hadn't been on that beach." She sounded enthusiastic and not like it was out of gratitude or anything.

"No way, Slim, a deal is a deal. I promised I'd buy you a steak dinner, and that's just what I'm going to do. How's six?"

"Perfect, I'll see you then." She really did look good. She looked much more… I don't know…alive? When I saw her in the hospital, she was not only close to death, but wanted it. Now she looked like she wanted to live. That made me happy. I checked with the Inn to make sure I didn't need a jacket for dinner. I'm not quite sure what came over me, but I felt the time was right to change my look.

I'd been out with lots of women before, but the kind of women I dated usually were the biker chick type. Most had as many tattoos as I did, some had more. They were the type of woman that could open a beer bottle with their teeth. They could give you a good fight in arm wrestling too. That's about it for their good qualities. Those rich girls that hung around bikers, they were just looking for cheap thrills and they didn't interest me. A night on the town with a biker chick was usually to a diner or burger joint. Slim wasn't like that, that's why I wanted tonight to be different. I just wanted tonight to be special for her. I wanted to make her want to keep on living. Even though I didn't need a jacket, I decided to take a ride into Bedford and buy some pants and a nice long-sleeved button-down shirt. I had only brought jeans and tee shirts up with me. I stopped by a barbershop and had him shave me bald and chop off the goatee leaving just the mustache. I had to admit I looked damn good.

I went back to the room to shower and change. I even borrowed a little of Jason's hoity-toity cologne. With my new duds and my new look, I was looking damn fine. I walked over to the Concord Academy where she was staying. As I walked up the path to the front door there was this rose bush with these beautiful peach colored roses, so I decide to hack one off for Slim. She was going to meet me outside, because you needed some kind of special key code to get in the place. When she came outside, I was sitting on the front porch snipping the thorns off the rose with my Swiss Army knife. When I saw her, I put the knife away, stood up and handed her the rose. She looked really pretty. She had on this flowy dress, which was good for someone as small as her to wear since it didn't hug that boney frame. It gave her some substance, but it was also feminine and soft looking.

"Thank you, Rico, what a beautiful rose. You look great! What a change from this morning…. not that I didn't like the way you looked this morning…I mean you looked fine; you just look really nice now too!" Nice recovery, I thought. I like a girl who can think on her feet.

"I thought this rose was nice, but I like wildflowers better, in fact Thoreau has a quote about wildflowers that I always liked, '

"Where the most beautiful wildflowers grow, there men's spirit is fed, and poets grow."

She seemed a bit amazed that I knew this quote.

"Rico, that's one of my favorite quotes…how did you know?"

"I didn't, it's just one of mine too. I guess we think alike. It's a beautiful night, do you mind walking?" I asked even though the only options were to ask her to drive, or put her on the back of the Sportster.

"No, I don't mind at all. Back home I walk all over Brigantine. There are

82

nice wide sidewalks." She seemed a tiny bit nervous, but not about being out with me, just like she was trying to impress me! Imagine that!

"I should slow down more and walk. Seeing everything from a Harley gives you only quick glimpses. Walking lets you see the details in things.

"In short, all good things are wild and free." Henry David Thoreau

"You actually are a Thoreau fan, aren't you?"

"Yeh, I've read most of his stuff. I like the way he writes and what he writes about. Are you surprised?"

"Yes, but not shocked. I can see there is a lot more to you than meets the eye. You march to your own drummer."

I nearly tripped in the road and fell flat on my face. I couldn't believe she described me that way. That was always how I felt about myself and it seems like I've always waited for the day when someone would just accept me for who I am, and realize that I hear a different drummer, and his music ain't so bad. Lucy was the only one who ever understood that about me and didn't try to change me. She accepted me for who I was. Maybe she knew there was good in me, so it didn't matter to her how I looked to other people. Maybe Slim sees the good in me. I see something in her too. I think she's just been waiting to be discovered. She's like a little tiny plant that's been covered up with dead leaves and can't quite grow big because it can't see the sun. It partly is praying for someone to remove the blanket of leaves so it can grow and flourish, and partly hoping the leaves stay just where they are so it doesn't risk being scorched by the sun. There's a danger in exposing yourself. Sometimes I guess it's easier to just hide yourself and deprive yourself of nutrients while you slowly wither away and become one again with the earth.

We got to the Inn and I asked her if she would rather sit inside or outside. She chose outside, which made me happy since that would have been my first preference. She seemed really comfortable being out with me, and I was with her.

"So, what looks good, Slim?" I asked her as she studied the menu.

"I think I'll have the Caesar salad."

"Ok, and what else?"

"That's it."

"No way. This is a steak dinner, not a rabbit food dinner. T-bone or Filet Mignon?"

"No, really" Then she leaned closer to me and whispered, "It's kind of expensive here."

I leaned a little closer still. My lips were practically touching her ear. Her pretty red hair would move a little with each puff of breath from me. I told her this was my treat and I wanted to see her enjoy a nice steak. I also told her this was not going to bankrupt me, since I am a low maintenance guy who makes a really good living, and I ain't hurting for money.

"I'm sorry. I didn't mean to imply…"

"Slim, please order a nice meal. I want to do this for you. Just relax. Don't worry about anything tonight. This is a celebration that you're still here on this planet"

"In that case, I'll have the filet mignon!"

"That's my girl!" After I said it, I almost wanted to grab it out of the air and stuff it back into my big fat mouth, but in a way, I was glad I said it too. It felt good to call her my girl. Maybe it would feel good to have a girl.

She looked like she was getting comfortable with me. She wasn't put off at all by the way I look. Even though I had toned it down for tonight, there were still a few tattoos exposed, and I had left my earrings in. She wasn't looking at the outside me, though, I could tell. She was only seeing the inside me. That's the "me" nobody ever sees, and I rarely show anyone either. I felt connected to her, maybe it had something to do with saving her off that beach in Brigantine. Maybe I had saved her for myself and not just for her sake.

Lucy Chapter 16

The months flew by and soon my beautiful baby girl was born. Billy and I were so happy! She had daddy wrapped around her tiny finger from the moment she made her appearance in the world. Her Uncle Rico was in love with her. She also immediately won my mother's stony heart. In the back of my mind I thought that once the baby was born, all would be forgiven, and it seemed as though it was. Mom even volunteered to baby sit on occasion. I named the baby "Olivia." Just like an olive branch I wanted her appearance to bring peace to my family. She looked so angelic and fragile. She was born with a mess of black hair and these big blue eyes that turned brown a few days after she was born. She needed so much love and attention. My life had changed forever, but I could never see resenting her the way Mom resented having me and Rico. I would dedicate my life to making the best possible world for my little girl, and she would never feel the rejection or disapproval my mother had for me.

Billy had controlled his temper through the pregnancy. I know it was hard for him. He had so much on his mind. He was taking the LSAT's to try to get into law school and of course the time of the test coincided with the birth of Olivia, so it was more stress for him. He was afraid to have sex with me while I was pregnant. I thought that he found me repulsive, but he said he was just worried about hurting the baby. He kept asking when the doctor said it would be time for us to resume activity again. The delivery went great so the doctor said to wait six weeks and then we could go back to normal. He also cautioned that even though I was breast-feeding, to make sure we used protection because I could be ovulating.

Truthfully, my only focus was Olivia. I loved Billy, and took care of him, but most of my energies were focused on her. I was fortunate she was born in May right after the semester ended, so I could spend three glorious months with her all to myself. She was such a good baby. She hardly ever cried and was just pleasant all the time. It was still exhausting taking care of an infant, and I found myself totally drained each day. But did we have fun together! We played every day, I took her for very long walks, and I read to her constantly. Her Uncle Rico spoiled her with attention and gifts, and he had a knack to quiet her when she got fussy. We would walk to the park and I would take some of my favorite authors from some of my English Lit courses and read out loud to her on a park bench. People must have thought I was crazy to be reading Shakespeare, Thoreau and Chaucer to an infant, but it really didn't matter what I was saying as long as I was holding her and speaking to her in soft tones.

I started to get to know some of the other mothers in the neighborhood who I would meet up with on my walks, but I did not have too much in common with them because of our age differences. Most were in their thirties and some even my mom's age. They looked at me with a bit of skepticism that I was only twenty-one, and they also tended to talk down to me, even though we were all new mothers and all in the same boat. Then what started to happen was that they all had to go back to work, and I was the only full-time mother. When I would meet up with the moms on the weekends, they started to have a new respect for me, since I seemed to be the one with the best baby, the most content and happy. Soon they were asking me for advice and showing me a bit more respect. One woman, Sarah, even said to me that I was a natural born mother. She had three older kids and she was one of the few mothers who was turning into a friend. She said some women are born mothers, others learn it, and some never do. The ones who are born mothers are rare and that I was one of them. That made me feel so good. To this day, I have never forgotten her words. When things got rough, I would remember her kind words, and know that my instincts would just get me through whatever I was facing. I believe that God sends you people to fill a certain need in your life, and He sent me Sarah to let me know I was doing okay, and I had made the right choice.

Billy was getting more and more anxious as the six weeks were almost over. I personally could have waited another six weeks. My long walks had melted the baby weight off, but I still felt different. My body had changed in subtle ways, and I wasn't quite comfortable with the changes yet. One evening before Billy got home, Olivia was taking a nap. She was on a set routine and would take an hour and a half nap around four o'clock every day. That usually gave me time to prepare dinner, but tonight, we were just having leftovers, so I had some time to myself. I decided to be totally indulgent and take a nice hot bath. My bathroom was just steps away from her crib so if she woke early, no problem. I drew the water and tossed in some bubble liquid that my cousin brought me in the hospital. She told me not to forget to take care of myself.

I was completely relaxed for the first time in I couldn't remember how long, when I heard the basement door open, and Billy called for me.

"I'm in the bathroom."

"Can I come in?"

"I'm just taking a bath." I really did not want or need company.

"A bath? You never take baths."

"I know, I just felt like relaxing."

"You smell so good…" He was starting to take off his clothes. "This was such a great idea!" He started to ease his way into the tub with me. I was annoyed at the intrusion. I just wanted to be by myself. He started kissing me and had positioned himself so he was on top of me. He was kissing me harder and thrusting himself inside me. I was trying to make him stop, but the tub was small, and we were wedged in tightly. He was kissing me so forcefully; I couldn't open my mouth. I could barely breathe. My head hurt from the hard porcelain beneath it, and I felt only fear, no pleasure. When he was done, he got out of the tub, dried off and asked what was for dinner. Too stunned to speak, I just wanted to stay in the warm water which felt safe even though I had just been violated in it. I could not believe what had just happened. I hadn't invited him into my tub, or into my body, he just barged right in. My feelings were a mix of fury, hurt, and confusion.

Olivia started to stir, and he said he would get her. My first instinct was to keep this animal away from my daughter, but if I caused a scene he would just get violent, and right now someone needed to tend to the baby, I was in no shape to do it. Slowly I got out of the tub and reached for my robe behind the door. I locked the door so I would have some privacy, and silently started to cry. How could Billy be so sweet sometimes, but so horrible other times? This was not how I wanted to spend the rest of my life. I was a good mother; I could get some sort of job after school that would support me and Olivia and could make it on my own if I left him. I had to start giving this some serious thought. For now, I would get dressed, and go take care of my baby.

Olivia was nearly three months old when I had to go back to school. Aunt Kris had just had her baby and she agreed to watch Olivia two days, my mother watched her one day. I arranged my classes so I was only at school three days, and because I had always taken extra classes, I was able to finish by Christmas. The fall flew by. It was very hectic trying to juggle motherhood and my schoolwork, but because of my support system I was able to do it. Through it all I still hadn't gotten a regular period yet and thought I should go to the doctor to make sure everything was all right.

I found out right before Thanksgiving that I was pregnant again. The doctor said I had to have gotten pregnant less than six weeks after giving birth and he scolded me since he told me not to have relations until the six-week check-up. I was too ashamed to tell him that it was not my choice and my husband had forced himself on me. I was delighted, but fearful. Here we go again. How would the family take this news? The shock had just started to wear off from my pregnancy with Olivia, I was about to finish college and be able to actually support myself and maybe get out of this hellish marriage, and now I was going to have another baby.

The doctor saw my look of bewilderment and said to me softly, "You know you have options"

I immediately snapped out of the place my mind had been going and told him point blank, "No, there is no option for me other than to have this baby, and I am truly happy, just shocked." I even managed a smile.

I was thinking about Billy just starting law school and the kind of pressure having another mouth to feed would put on him. I was thinking about my mother and how much she would hate me now, and once again think I was irresponsible. I was thinking about all the mothers in town and how they would look at me. I was thinking about Olivia and how unfair it was that she would have to share my attention with another baby. I constantly thought about the way this baby was conceived. I was thinking about a million things, but for all my thinking I did not know how this would affect me.

I went straight from the doctor's office to church with Olivia strapped in her snuggly sack close to my chest, feeling each other's heartbeats. She was the kind of baby I could take with me into doctor's offices and churches and not fear her making a fuss. She was just happy to be out and close to me.

Father Joe happened to be in the rectory today. He was about my height, with a very pleasant round face and a kindly bald head. Hair just somehow would not have looked right on him. He had a gentle manner and never sounded in brimstone, only love and forgiveness and joy. He was always a great comfort to me. He was the priest who Christened Olivia, and married Billy and me. He was my confessor and my friend, and I turned to him when I needed someone to talk to. For most things I could turn to Rico, but anything involving my marriage I had to keep from Rico because I knew there was one thing that would light his fuse and that was thought of anyone hurting me. So here I was again going before Father Joe with one of my sad stories.

"Come in Lucy, let me hold that beautiful baby of yours." As if she knew this was a good and holy person, Olivia stretched out her precious chubby little arms to Father Joe as he scooped her up gently in his. "This is such a treat. I didn't know I would get to see my Olivia today!"

"Father, I'm afraid I've done it again…"

"What have you done, my dear?"

"I'm pregnant."

"That's wonderful! Oh, what happy news! Are you not happy?"

"Yes Father, I'm very happy. I love being a mother and will welcome a new baby with open arms, I'm just so scared that everyone will react the same way they did to my pregnancy with Olivia."

"How did Billy react?"

"He doesn't know yet, Father, you and my doctor are the first to know."

"I take it you two were not trying purposely to conceive again." I couldn't fight back the tears anymore. The memories of the night this baby was conceived just flooded back to me. "What's wrong child?"

"Billy forced himself on me. I wasn't ready to start sleeping with him again, and he was…"

"Oh, my dear, how awful for you." He paused for a moment, "How are things now between the two of you?"

"Well, since he started Law School, he has been too busy to think about sex. His temper has been flaring up quite a bit because of the pressures. I keep thinking, and God forgive me, that I would be better off raising my daughter alone, but now with two babies I don't know if I can do it."

"You are considering divorce?"

"Yes, father, I know it is against church rules, but I don't think I want my children growing up in a household where their father hurts their mother."

"The church has no such rule that says you must remain in a marriage where your safety is compromised. Let us pray a bit for guidance and for strength." We paused a moment to silently send our thoughts on this subject up to God. Then Father Joe spoke again. "Lucy, you are so young. You are just twenty-one, and you have been through so much. God is watching over you. He sent you this precious gift in Olivia, and now, because of your goodness, and obvious flair at motherhood, he is rewarding you with a second beautiful baby. You are a favorite child of his, I know this is true. These children will bring you great joy and happiness in the years to come, and will be the answer to the question 'why me?' They are the reason why you must go through the pain you are now experiencing, and the strength you will get after you go through these rough times will make it all worthwhile."

I could feel the tears forming in the back of my eyes and a lump in my throat. He must have sensed it too. He took my hand and spoke directly at me. Even Olivia stopped squirming and just stared up at me as he spoke. "Lucy, God has chosen you for a special purpose. You are an exceptional woman with an incredible capacity to love and be loved. You are going to inspire multitudes of people someday with your great hope, and optimism, and sheer goodness. This will all pass one day, but the mark you leave on this earth will remain. It will remain through your children, and through the goods works you do."

"Father, you are the best!" I was relieved that Father Joe understood my reasons for wanting to divorce Billy. I was also so flattered that he thought I was chosen for a special purpose. I intuitively know that everything happens for a reason. Sometimes you need to be reminded of that. I knew this would all work out. I would be fine. "Thank you for making me feel better."

"Lucy, it is your incredible faith that is making you feel better. I am just reminding you to tap into it because it lies there waiting for you."

'Thank you, father." I left the church as always feeling better than when I came. I got enough encouragement from Father Joe to be able to face the tough times ahead.

Billy Chapter 17

I tried to be a good husband while Lucy was pregnant and when she presented me with that beautiful baby girl my heart melted. She had Lucy's big beautiful brown eyes and was just as calm and sweet as her mother. I fell as hard and fast for her as I had for Lucy, but I vowed I would never hurt my Olivia the way I hurt her mother. I was studying so hard during the last few months of Lucy's pregnancy, and she was so big I didn't dare go near her sexually, so I was pretty excited when I came home one night a few weeks after the baby was born and found Lucy in the bathtub. Before I knew it, I had climbed in with her and I was coming inside her. I guess I didn't realize until I finished that she was crying and didn't seem as excited about having sex at that moment as I was. I did not want to deal with her, so I just left the bathroom, threw on some clothes and got Olivia up from her nap.

My inability to keep it in my pants resulted in Lucy getting pregnant again. How could she do this to me?

Ted Chapter 18

At work I began to notice this girl who was different than any girl I had ever seen down on the farm. She was what the old timers might call a painted woman. She wore lots of make-up, fake eyelashes, tight bright clothes, and high heeled shoes. And this was to work every day! I wondered how she dressed when she went out on the town? I thought she was gorgeous. I was totally intrigued by her. I asked around and found out her name was Sharon. I had to get to know her, but I was painfully shy.

I tossed and turned all night thinking of how I might approach her. The next day I was exhausted and couldn't focus on work. I remember thinking I would sell my soul to the devil if I could have Sharon. At that moment my exhaustion must have gotten the best of me and I must have dozed off at my desk for a moment. I woke up what could not have been more than a few seconds later in a cold sweat with a very strange feeling in my chest. Almost as if my heart had been ripped out. My head was pounding, but I also felt strangely invigorated and as if I had the courage to approach Sharon. It was 12:00 noon, time for lunch. I found her in the company cafeteria.

"Hi, aren't you Sharon that works in administration?"

"Yes, and you're Ted from IT."

"Wow, you know my name?" I felt like such an idiot after I said it, but she put me right at ease with her response.

"Of course, my friends told me this guy from IT keeps asking people about me. You probably know more about me now than I do!" We both gave a nervous laugh. When she parted her lips, I could see that her teeth were really crooked. It was one of those things you wonder for a split second if it will bother you, but I decided I was so smitten, it wouldn't. We talked for a few more minutes about work related stuff and people we knew from the company, and when it was time for her to get back to work, I asked her if I could call her sometime. She said okay and gave me her number. I went back to my cubby on a cloud and immediately used the reverse directory to find her address. I called the local florist and had a dozen roses sent to her house with a note asking if we could go out on Friday.... this was Tuesday; I thought a three-day warning was sufficient. I called her later that night to see if she got the flowers. She said she did, and that she had plans for Friday. I was crushed! How could she not want to go out with me after that fabulous gesture? Then she asked if Saturday was okay with me. I was so shocked I nearly dropped the receiver.

"Sure, Saturday is fine. Can we go out to eat? What kind of food do you like? Do you have a favorite restaurant?" I was rambling. "I should probably shut up now."

She giggled again, and then said, "I just don't like Mexican. Anything else is fine" I was kind of hoping for a little more enthusiasm, but maybe she was just nervous too. I decided I had to have her, and I was going to win her over no matter what I had to do.

"Let's go to Alabaster's," I blurted out.

"Are you serious? That's the most expensive restaurant in town!"

"I've heard the food is phenomenal and it is a beautiful setting. It would probably be a nice place to get to know each other."

"Great!" She replied. I sensed a lot more enthusiasm in her voice now.

"How is 7:00?"

"Make it 7:30."

"Done." I said.

"Okay, see you Saturday!" As I hung up the phone, my hands were all sweaty. I had such an adrenaline rush just talking to her on the phone. Saturday night would be fabulous. I wondered what she would wear. She always looked so hot at work with her tight clothes and high heels. I was sure she would tone it down a bit for a place like Alabasters and not look so…what's the word I'm looking for? Trashy? I could tell she would wear the appropriate outfit for the occasion, but what would that be? Maybe some sophisticated suit or a tailored coat dress with just the right slit to make it look provocative without being embarrassing. Or maybe some sexy sweater dress that showed off her curves without being too revealing. Whatever she would wear I knew I would not be able to concentrate on anything but what was under it anyway. I am bad that way. When I look at a beautiful woman, I can't stop thinking about what lies beneath her clothing. Is she wearing silk or satin, or even some lace? Okay, I had done enough thinking now on that subject. If I didn't stop now, I would never get to sleep tonight.

The days crawled that week as I waited for Saturday to come. As luck would have it, I was doing an off-site project for the remainder of the week, so I wasn't even able to bump into her in the cafeteria. I thought about calling to confirm Saturday, but I thought I might look foolish, like I was afraid she would back out or something.

Finally, the day came. I decided I would wear my blue pinstriped suit. It was my nicest one, and I had just had it cleaned so it smelt pretty good too. I vacillated between about half a dozen other choices and was proud of myself for making my decision in under an hour. Most decisions I make take much longer than that. My next hard choice would be what

97

shirt to wear. I'm not a very big guy, about 5'9" around 170 lbs. I probably only have a 15 ½ "neck but I always buy my shirts in a size 16 ½ because I can't stand to have anything tight around my neck. I feel like I am choking. I tie my neckties a little on the loose side for the same reason. I still thought I looked damn good!

I drove up to her house in my Dodge Neon. I was on my way as far as my career was concerned; I wasn't quite there yet. I always kept my car very clean, so at least it wasn't embarrassing. It would still be a few more years before I could afford a really nice car. For now, I leased the Neon, because I just didn't want to commit to a car when in a few years I could probably afford something nicer. I tend to think like that. I hesitate making any major purchases because I never know how I am going to feel about it down the road or if something better will come out and I will be stuck with the thing I chose.

Her house was really disheveled. The yard had some dying bushes, and the driveway had an old rotting car that reminded me of one of the field cars we used to have on the farm. I learned to drive in a field car. Dad used to pick up at auction these cheap, dilapidated cars and we would fix them up just enough so that we could use them in the back forty. You couldn't take a field car on the road because it wasn't plated. They were strictly used to get us out to the fields a little faster.

The bell on the front door was broken and I started to use the doorknocker when Sharon came to the door. I had a bouquet of wildflowers that I had picked up at the same florist I had sent the roses from. When she came to the door, I could see past her into a hazy smoke-filled living room with two people sitting on the couch watching Wheel of Fortune and chain smoking.

"Mom, Dad, this is Ted Harmon." I extended my hand to each of them, but they barely took their eyes off the TV. I could tell this was bad timing. Pat was done with his introductions and Vanna was itching to turn some letters. Velda from Cincinnati had won the toss backstage and was about to do the first spin. By the suffocating cloud of smoke and the amount of cigarette butts in the ashtray I could see these people were heavy chain smokers. The lung-exposing cough her mother produced after I shook her hand confirmed that. I didn't want to be rude, but I really needed to get out of that place fast. The smell was making me sick and I didn't want the disgusting smell of old cigarettes to linger on me all night. Sharon reappeared with the flowers in a vase and set them down on the living room coffee table next to the filthy ashtray. I could actually see the flowers wilting from the smoke. I looked at my watch and said something along the lines of how we had a reservation and should be going yada yada yada.

Once we got out into the fresh air, I realized that indeed the smell was lingering on me, and worse yet, it was on her too. I guess even more so on her since she actually lives in that house. I put that thought away because for the first time I actually realized where I was! I was where I had dreamed of being all week. Out with the girl of my dreams and fantasies. For the first time since escaping the house of horrors, I took a look at her. I hoped she didn't notice the dismay in my eyes at her choice of outfits. She was wearing a mini skirt that was way too tight, and a top that exposed her midriff. I thought she could have looked better. All I could say, very diplomatically I thought was, "It's gotten really chilly, you should really put on something a little warmer" I thought this would make me look as though I was only concerned with her welfare rather than my embarrassment over her choice of outfits.

"You're probably right, I'll go get my jacket" She started to go in the house and asked me if I wanted to wait inside with her parents. I quickly said no, I didn't want to disturb their show again, so I would wait right here. When she emerged from the house, she had on this dyed pink rabbit fur short jacket. I could barely believe it. She looked like a hooker from a bad rerun of Starsky and Hutch. I know her tacky dressing is what first attracted me to her, but come on, this was Alabasters! She could have at least tried to dress normally.

I decided I wouldn't let this bother me. I was just going to enjoy being out with her and get to know what all her good qualities were. She had some nice qualities. She wasn't much in the brains department, but she had this really good body. She wasn't all that pretty as the night wore on and the make-up started to wear off, but she had this really great body. I decided that night I would marry her.

I don't know what came over me. I'm not usually one to make a quick decision; but my mind was made up. I wanted to have a family someday, and the only way I could have children to care for me in my old age was to find a wife, and she was as good a candidate as anyone.

Eventually, I brought her up to the farm to meet my family. They were not impressed, and neither was she with them. She came to the farm in high heels, which was an immediate black mark against her with my folks. They were hoping to show her around the farm, but her obvious disdain for getting dirty and being outside was a definite problem.

She thought they were too loud and overwhelming. Well, there are a lot of us Harmons and I guess we can be overwhelming, but if she was going to be a Harmon she would have to get used to it. My folks tried to talk me out of marrying her, in a very subtle way of course, but since my mind was made up, I was going through with it. I got her a beautiful ring that she absolutely adored, and the wedding plans began. Fortunately, I needed to have nothing at all to do with the planning. Sharon and her mom told me all I had to do was show up on the day of the wedding, and they would take care of everything. Fine with me.

I bought us a nice little house in South Salem with lots of property around it. The house was small, but it was the land that sold it for me. I can't be too close to my neighbors. I don't want to hear them sneeze. This house was perfect. It had a little stream running through the back yard and was a short walk to the lake. The picture was almost complete. I had the house, the wife, now the next piece of the pie was the kids. We didn't really talk about having kids before we got married, so I assumed it was just a given. After all, that is just how it is done. You get married, you have kids, your kids take care of you in your old age. That's that.

I was shocked and stunned the day Sharon told me she didn't want to have children. She wanted to work and just travel and have fun with me. We got into a big argument because I told her it was extremely important to me to have children. I spoke to her mother about it. I knew she could convince her that the time was right to start a family. Fortunately, between commercial breaks on Wheel of Fortune, Mom was able to convince Sharon that if she didn't want to have children, I was going to leave her. One month later she was pregnant.

I always said that it was me and my mother-in-law that had the baby. Sharon was extremely distant, and her maternal instincts really weren't kicking in. I loved every minute of fatherhood and loved my baby girl. I couldn't wait to have more children. We went through the whole 'if we don't have another baby, I'm leaving you' thing and soon baby number two was on the way.

I was ecstatic. I was the greatest dad ever. I didn't mind sharing anything, including my pumpkin with my two baby girls. There was nothing I wouldn't do for them, after all, they were the little flowers in my garden that were going to take care of me one day. I had to treat them well now.

Sharon was getting increasingly depressed. I was working long hours to make a good life for my girls to try to pick up the slack since I made her quit her job. It wasn't like she was bringing in such a great amount of money as a secretary, and she didn't have too much earning potential. She graduated with a degree from a vocational training program. It was the kind of program they send kids to who just aren't bright enough to make it in a regular classroom situation, so they put them in such a program so that they may become productive members of society. I forget what she studied there; I don't know basket weaving or something.

She would wait for me to come home every night and just throw the girls at me and go up to our bedroom and not come out until morning. Sometimes when I went upstairs, I found her in the bathroom plucking out her eyelashes. It grossed me out so much, I could barely look at her. This went on until the oldest, Liza, started preschool. Having only one baby to take care of seemed to make things a little better for her, but she was still miserable. One day I got a frantic call from my mother-in-law saying Sharon had dropped the kids off there at noon and said she'd be back in an hour, and it was now 4:00 and she hadn't heard from her. I left work and rushed over to her house. This was very unusual. Sharon knows I never wanted her mother to watch the girls in that disgusting smoke-filled house, if my mother-in-law ever watches the girls it's in our house and she is forbidden from smoking around them. "Where did she say she was going, Mom?"

"She didn't, Ted, she just said she'd be back in an hour! I'm so worried, I don't know what to do."

"I'll start calling the police and the local hospitals." I made a few phone calls and called all her friends. No one had heard anything from her. Around 9:00 that night the phone rang. It was Sharon.

"Ted, I can't take this life anymore. I had to get away. I just need a few days by myself. I'll call you tomorrow."

She didn't call the next day. A few days turned into a few weeks, into a few months. No one knew where she was, not her mother, not her friends, no one. I kept trying to figure out what I did wrong. We had such a picture-perfect life. A beautiful home, two beautiful children, money to do things like vacations, how could she have been so unhappy? Finally, after two months, she came home. I never really asked her where she was or what she was doing. I just assumed that since she came back, she was ready to resume our normal life.

She seemed happier, for a while. She wanted me to spend more time with her, but I was always too busy at work, and when I was home, I wanted to be with the girls. Almost a year to the day from her disappearing act, she served me with divorce papers. I was told to stay out of the house and kept away from my girls. How could this be happening? I was such a good father and good provider. Why was she so angry with me? What had I done? I figured the only way I was ever going to be able to have a relationship with my girls was to be nice to her. I didn't fight her. I was almost afraid to. She was scary. There was just something almost demonic about her. I didn't want to rock the boat with her. I paid all the bills, I gave her everything she asked for and wanted, and she rewarded me by allowing me to have the girls every weekend. I was still so devastated. I started to retreat into a world that let no one in except my girls. I saw no friends, or family. I didn't date at all. I just worked, slept, ate, and lived for the weekends.

I began to hear the rumors all over town that she had many boyfriends. She was always seen with a new guy. The girls would even tell me about times they encountered one of mommy's 'friends' having breakfast with them in his pajamas. I thought this was her way of trying to make me jealous. I let her do her thing. I just didn't want to confront her, because any time I did she would fly off the handle and threaten to keep the girls from me. Of course in a heartbeat I could have had the girls taken from her because of the disappearing stunt she pulled, but that would mean they would have to come live with me, and I still thought a mother who was home with them was better than a father who worked all the time. So, she was holding all the cards and she knew it.

I wanted to be back in my house. She was letting it fall into such disrepair. She was a slob. There was garbage piled up all over the place and no room to move around. It was never like this when I lived there. I'm something of a neat freak and I kept everything in its proper place. As the girls got older, they were embarrassed to have their friends come over to their mom's house for play dates. They would usually wait until the weekend and have their friends come to my apartment. My apartment was fun. I had a big screen TV, a huge pit of a couch, and outside there was lots of room to romp around. It wasn't quite the one hundred acres I grew up on, but it was about six nice suburban acres. I moved several times during the separation. I never really like to stay in one place too long. This apartment was a rental with no lease, which was perfect for me. When the mood hit me, I could pack up and move again. I felt that since I was still paying off the mortgage and the taxes on the house in South Salem, I would just rent and not be saddled with two mortgages. Sharon never pressed me to sign the divorce papers. She was content to have me out of the house and yet still financially responsible for her.

There was a girl, Laurie, who rented the apartment below me. We became good friends, but there was no romantic involvement at all. We spent a great deal of time together with the kids. She had a girl and a boy that were around the same ages as my girls, so it was nice to have companionship. Word got back to their mom that I had a female friend and all of a sudden Sharon was interested in me again. She started calling just to say "Hi." She started coming around, when normally, I always had to pick the girls up, she would never go out of her way to bring them to me. Eventually she told me she wanted to reconcile and for us to be a family again. I told her I would give it a shot. We almost made a go of it.

We decided we would start on equal footing, so we would fix up the house in South Salem then put it on the market and buy a new house to have a fresh start.

We never even got to the point when we could live together. The sheer stress of trying to clean out the pigsty she had created proved to be too much for us to handle and we ended up fighting all the time. The girls were devastated. They had really hoped we would be a family again and it broke my heart to have to tell them that it just wasn't going to work.

I went back to my solitary life feeling very defeated and deflated. It took a very long time and much therapy before the girls could recover from this. Sharon went back to her boy toys. It always amazed me how popular she was with men since she never lost all the weight she gained when she was carrying Nancy. Laurie moved away, and a single guy moved in downstairs. I wasn't much into socializing, and he was pretty quiet, so it suited me just fine. I had a few blind dates, but nothing serious. Of course, it got reported back to Sharon that I was dating, and she was all over me again. I decided to give reconciliation another shot since the holidays were coming up and it would be so nice to be a family for Thanksgiving and Christmas. We didn't even make it to the turkey leftovers. Once again, the girls were devastated. My family was really getting annoyed with me. They never really liked Sharon and couldn't understand why I kept going back to her, getting the girls hopes up and then pulling away. I couldn't really understand it either. I guess it could have been a bit of guilt, or a bit of obligation or a sense that I wanted to do the right thing for my girls, but I just kept screwing up. I felt like I couldn't control my actions. I felt like there were some invisible hands pushing me to do things I knew I shouldn't do, but somehow felt pressured and compelled to do.

Lucy Chapter 19

As predicted, the reaction to my second pregnancy was not well received. Billy flew off the handle and called me a stupid bitch and whined about how hard his life was going to be now that he was in law school and had another baby to feed. The only reason he did not get physical with me was because Olivia was sleeping peacefully in the snuggly sack attached to me. I was not even going to get into the argument that this would not have happened if he had been patient and had not forced himself on me.

My mother reacted in a similar way. She told me I was selfish and irresponsible again. I was not going to tell her that her precious lawyer son-in-law raped his wife. I decided I would take the higher road. I also didn't want my baby to ever find out he or she was conceived in a forceful way, not out of love and tenderness. I saw nothing good coming of me telling my mother any of this, so I just didn't. My only supportive family member, as always was Rico who gave me a big bear hug, patted my belly and gave me that wink that spoke volumes of love and support. Through his rough exterior, Mohawk haircut, and odd piercings and tattoos, Rico's heart always was visible to the naked eye.

My second baby was a little boy that we named Joseph Enrico after Father Joe and Rico. He too was a good sleeper, but he was a bit more rambunctious than Olivia and I really had my hands full. Olivia was just under a year old when she was presented with her brother. She was a smart little girl, strong and agile. She started walking at 10 months which was a real lifesaver and back saver for me. I would still carry her a lot, but it was great knowing I could carry the baby in one arm, and she could walk beside me holding my free hand.

My in-laws gave us a double stroller as a baby gift and I continued to spend my days walking, and reading to my babies, and making new friends in the park. The summer that Joey was an infant was very tight financially. Billy was entering his second year of law school... that is known as the year they work you to death. He was working during the day in a bank and going to school at night, so I didn't see him much. He wasn't making much money, so we were in dire straits. I figured we would have enough money to pay the bills, but come September, any savings we had would be dried up and I would need to think of a way to bring in more money.

Through high school and college, I had worked in a Candy Shop on the boardwalk in Asbury Park. They specialized in making homemade chocolates. I had picked up quite a few tips while working there, and often would make chocolate party favors for friends and family. Sarah asked me if I would make the party favors for her oldest daughters Communion party. I told her I would love to. She insisted on paying me. At first, I refused, but she was adamant.

I loved making chocolate. It was something I was able to do in my own kitchen, and Olivia and Joey's good sleeping habits afforded me ample time to complete my projects. I decided to make roses out of white chocolate and tied them with white tulle and arranged them in a basket. They served as both a centerpiece and party favors. At the end of the party the little communion girl handed each guest a chocolate rose from the basket. It was a huge hit. Sarah had invited close to seventy-five people. From that party, 20 people called me to tell me how clever they thought the favors were, as well as beautiful and delicious. My career as a chocolatier was born.

This was perfect for me. I was able to stay home with my babies and still make some good money. The only down time was the summer, other than that I was operational from September through May. I made party favors as well as holiday gifts. I started building a clientele that were loyal and devoted to my chocolates.

I decided my candy making was the way to go since working outside the home was near impossible. I got very aggressive with my advertising. I had relied on word of mouth, but I enhanced it but printing up cards that didn't cost much and making flyers that I stuck in each bag of chocolate I delivered. My clientele started to grow. I also felt the best way to get new customers was to have them taste my chocolate. I would send chocolate with anyone I knew who worked in a large office in the hopes it would generate some more business.

This worked once again through my good friend and guardian angel, Sarah. Her husband took in a box of dollar sign-shaped chocolates to work. He worked for an investment banking company. They were such a hit! His boss saw them and asked if I could make them and package them creatively for the company's big fiftieth anniversary party next month. He said they would be willing to spend around $5 a box for a favor! And they needed 300 favors! My head was spinning. I was doing the math as fast as I could in my heads...$1,500 total...cost to make was about $250...$1,250 in profit, and I could do it all in about a week! I combed through paper outlets and discount stores and found these adorable treasure chest boxes and filled them with dollar sign chocolate pieces. I wrapped them beautifully, and they were a smash hit. I had stickers made up with my name and number and stuck one to the bottom of each favor. I called my business Chocolations. It was just a word I made up combining 'chocolate' and 'celebrations.' This was the beginning of what would be a very lucrative and successful business for me.

Quickly it became evident that I was going to have to move this business out of my own kitchen and find someplace else to work. Fortunately, now the kids had started preschool, so I could still work on my chocolate while they were in school and be around to pick them up. Just down the street from my parents' house was a little business district and I noticed sitting behind one of the buildings a small garage sized structure. It said 'for rent' so I started to make some inquiries. I found out that it had been used as an auxiliary kitchen for a bakery. With a few modifications I could turn it into my little chocolate warehouse and do my work there.

I kept so busy that I hardly had time to be in the line of fire with Billy, and this seemed to allow the marriage to hang on, though it was surely not a good one. As my business grew, he got more and more resentful of me. I always felt torn. He didn't like it when I made no money, but he seemed to like it even less when I was making money. He looked upon it as a hobby and not real work even though sometimes I would bring home favors to wrap and be up until three a.m. curling ribbons. Sometimes he would get his digs in and say, "when we met you were going to write the great American novel, and now you're peddling candy."

He worked for a small general practice firm in Long Branch. We were still in the basement at my mother's, because now we had all these law school loans to pay off, and his starting salary was nominal. It was really my chocolate business that was keeping food on the table and clothes on the kid's backs. It was not making us rich, but it certainly was keeping us off public assistance. My mother had grown close to the kids as I had prayed she would, but I felt as though her tolerance level of me was low. I sort of just came along as part of the package. She was still resentful and angry about what I did all these years later despite the wonderful outcome. I felt that the only way we could ever have a good relationship again was if I could somehow make a success of myself and show her that I hadn't thrown my life away. The fact that I was raising two beautiful, amazing children and running a business was not enough for her.

Right before Olivia was about to start kindergarten Billy was given the opportunity to go to New York to work for his firm's branch there. It would mean us moving, or me staying here and finally divorcing him. There was a part of me that wanted to cut the ties with him and just let him go alone, but there was another part of me that still loved him and remembered the good person he was and wanted to go to New York if for nothing else than to get a fresh start and get away from my mother and all her negativity. It was very scary, though. Part of what kept me in my mother and father's home was also the fact that I feared being alone with Billy. I didn't know what it would be like if he and I were in our own place and no one could hear me scream. Many a night when he went on the warpath, I figured the only thing keeping me alive was the fact that he knew my parents could hear. They never tried to stop him, but they could hear. He never dared try anything when Rico was around. If Rico were 100 miles away, could I ever feel safe?

I made up my mind. I would go to New York with Billy...then divorce him. This way, he could stay close to the kids, and I could have that fresh start I so desperately needed. I didn't tell him of my plan. I figured I would move up with him, and then have him served with papers. It was scary. I know that abusers get the most violent when they are served, but I was willing to take my chances if it meant I would finally have the peace I so desperately needed.

We found a cute little apartment in Eastchester right on Route 22. It had a storefront below it that was perfect for my chocolate shop. His firm was giving him a housing allowance, and I was able to take out a small business loan that enabled us to afford it. I decided I would move from just manufacturing to selling out of a storefront. It was all the space I needed. I had a nice little kitchen set up in the back and a small but workable showroom, with used cases I got at auction from a bakery going out of business. I added my homey touches, and *Chocolations Homemade Candies* was open for business!

The kids loved the store and their new home. Olivia fit right in at kindergarten and Joey loved his preschool. I brought them to school every morning and picked them up each afternoon. I had this very sweet retired grandmotherly type, Mary a retired schoolteacher, who worked in

110

the store, and covered for me when I ran to get the kids. I knew her from when I had worked at the candy shop in New Jersey. She was looking for a fresh start as well after losing her husband. She was a Godsend and having her around meant I could go upstairs and fix the kids lunch and play with them or bring them downstairs to "work" with me in the store. They loved it, and I loved having them there. It was a happy time for me, until Billy got home each night.

He was working long hours and was getting increasingly miserable at work. He was also studying for the New York Bar Exam that was coming up in February, and he had to pass in order to keep his job. He wasn't allowed to represent clients until he passed, so he was basically doing paralegal level work and getting increasingly frustrated as the days wore on.

When I met Billy he was a deep thinker. He was reading a lot and studying philosophy. I had been reading a great deal lately. I wanted to offer him some sort of encouragement. I wrote him a note and included in it my favorite Thoreau quote,

"In the long run, men hit only what they aim at. Therefore, though they should fail immediately, they better aim at something high."

That quote always meant so much to me. I wanted him to see that he would eventually reach his goals. He just had to keep trying and not lower his standards or expectations and never give up hope. As long as he continued to aim high, he would eventually get there. I hoped he would understand this. Instead he read the note, crumpled it up and threw it at me screaming, I don't need your sympathy, or your philosophy and I don't need to have my own wife calling me a failure!"

My mouth just hung open while at the same time I was bracing myself for his verbal blows to turn into physical ones. Sometimes it happened, sometimes it didn't. It was always hard to know when the time would be. I wanted to tell him that was not what I had meant at all. I did not see him as a failure, I saw him as a success for trying something so difficult. He just did not get it. It appeared that no matter what I said or did, it was the wrong thing. I just could not get through to him. It was as if we were two people from two different countries each speaking our native tongue and getting increasingly frustrated that we were not being understood. The only difference was I felt as though I was at least trying to understand him. It was as if I was reading the Berlitz *Learn Billy in Five Days* book and he was making no effort at all to learn my language.

In my study of the complex language of Billy I could see that the bar exam preparation was grueling, and I tried to make things as pleasant for him as I could. I decided it was not the best time to spring the divorce on him. He sailed through the New Jersey Bar exam, but this was New York. It was the hardest bar exam in the country and the February test had a notoriously low pass rate. Only about 47% of the people who take the exam in February pass it. If they fail, they then must wait until July when it is offered again. It seems unfathomable that in a country like ours that people who beat out probably nine other people for a spot in law school, who study hard for four years working day and night, saddle themselves with tens of thousands of dollars in loans, and have gotten an education with which they could actually do good and help people, are prevented from using their education just because they may not be good at taking a test. This is no ordinary test. It spans two days. It takes two months of intense day and night studying to prepare for; it requires that you memorize facts about laws that you will never use. It basically asks you to invent the law as you go along and does not give you time to write a reasoned and well thought out answer. In short, the process stinks, and as much as Billy can be a miserable human being at times, when it came to him griping about the bar exam, I could see his point. I also knew that a normal person would get stressed out over this, someone with a fuse as short as Billy's could explode at any moment. I tried to proceed with caution.

The exam was given the last Tuesday and Wednesday in February. It was held at the Jacob Javitz Center in Manhattan. Even though we were just about thirty-five minutes from Manhattan, his firm put him up in a hotel for the night before the exam and the night between exams. It's crucial with the February exam to be in the city, because if there should be a big snowstorm or some other act of God that keeps you from getting to the city, you have just blown two months of your life, and need to wait six more months before being able to take it again.

I prayed long and hard that Billy would pass this exam. He really needed this step up in pay for us to start getting back on our feet. If we separated it was going to be extremely hard for me to survive with the kids if he didn't have money to make support payments. We were lucky the chocolate shop was successful, Valentine's Day had been phenomenal, but it was always an adventure come bill-paying time. Sometimes we had money for the bills, sometimes we did not. Sometimes we would just make our bills and have to live on chocolate for the last few days of the month! I guess not the worst problem in the world.

It was getting a bit scary though since the summer was coming up. I would stay open for part of the summer, but there was no way I could be open in the hottest part of the summer. My chocolate would never survive. I would still have to pay all my bills even if the shop were closed, so if Billy had an income during that time, it would help.

He came home from the Javitz center looking like a man who had been released from prison. Relieved it was over, but not quite sure what to do with his freedom. He had been imprisoned studying for this exam for two months. Now he was out on parole. It wasn't over yet, now started the three-month waiting period until the results posted.

Surprisingly, I actually missed him while he was studying. I made him a nice dinner and even had a few little gifts for him when he got home. Nothing big, just little tokens so he would know I was thinking of him and wishing him well. Once he got used to being home again, the kids started jumping all over him and he started getting cranky. I tried to get them to stop, but they were so happy to see him after his long study period. He usually had a lot of patience with the kids, but tonight he was just too tired to deal with it, and I could see he was about to boil over. He always got a certain look in his eyes, his skin turned just a tinge red, and I could smell a different odor about him when he was about to blow. Once I saw the signs, I tried to keep things as calm as possible, and get out of the way before he erupted. I told the kids to wash up and get ready for bed.

"Can't you control those kids? I'm exhausted, I really can't deal with them jumping all over me!" He yelled.

I should have just kept my mouth shut, but I thought silence might also set him off, so I tried to explain. "They're just happy to see you, you've been gone for two days, and you've been studying for so long…"

"That's why I need some peace!" He shouted. I wasn't going to get into a screaming match with him, so I just turned to leave the room. "Don't you turn your back on me!!!!" He screamed.

Now I was getting upset. I didn't want him to frighten the children. "Please keep your voice down, I don't want the kids to hear you…" I said through clenched teeth.

"You're always so concerned about everybody hearing me, I don't care who hears me!!" That was obvious because he was yelling so loud, they could probably hear him back in New Jersey.

I could not take him yelling at me anymore. "That's it, Billy! I did nothing wrong tonight and everything in my power to make your homecoming pleasant, and all you have done is be nasty and scream at me. I've had it, I'm divorcing you!" I wished I could have taken it back, because I knew this was going to make him crazy and the timing of telling him the night of the bar exam was atrocious.

His eyes filled with tears and he grabbed me in a bear hug that was more strangling than loving "No, Lucy, you can't leave me, I love you, I love you more than anything. You love me too. You know you love me. You have to love me. Please, just forget this, just forget I said anything." I could feel his stinky hot breath on me, and felt his crocodile tears falling on the back of my neck.

I really had reached my limit with him, and even though I knew my troubles would be just starting, they had to start somewhere, so I pushed him off me and said, "No, I'm not going to live in fear or control anymore. I want you to leave."

His fury ignited "Well, I'm not going to fuckin leave. You, fuckin leave! This is my house and I'm not going anywhere." With that he slammed me against the wall so hard it knocked a shelf off the wall that was holding some dishes and they came crashing down to the floor shattering in a million pieces as I felt the shelf crash on my head. I was slipping in and out of consciousness, but I saw the flashing lights through the window, heard my children crying and saw Billy being taken away in handcuffs while they strapped me on the gurney.

I could hear Joey crying "no Mommy, don't die, please don't die!" Olivia just held my hand and would not let it go. I vaguely recall the police telling the kids they could ride in the police car to go see Mommy in the hospital and that I had just gotten a bad booboo on my head and I would be just fine. I also heard them praise Olivia for being such a brave, and smart young girl knowing how to dial 911.

Rico Chapter 20

My sister tries to keep me in the dark, but I knew something was wrong.
I questioned the kids without trying to scare them and from their answers
I knew something wasn't right with the story that Lucy fell and got a
concussion. Billy's a good guy, but I think he can be a hothead. If I find
out he had anything to do with this, I'll fuckin' kill him!

Lucy Chapter 21

The next few months were a living hell. Billy was trying desperately to win me back, but I was too hurt and angry to even give him the time of day. My forehead had a permanent scar near the hairline, and I was fully recovered from my concussion, but it was the emotional wounds that I was still nursing. I had a temporary restraining order on him, so at least he could not physically come near me, but he sent gifts and cards, and called. Eventually I had to have the order modified to say he could have no contact at all with the kids or me. I had to literally hold Rico back from trying to kill him or unleash his pals on him. I told him Billy couldn't hurt me anymore, and I didn't want the kids to go through any more confusion and pain.

Billy sent his brother from Boston to try to talk to me. I was not backing down. I heard from his brother that Billy was totally distraught because he failed the bar exam and could not see his kids and missed me terribly. He told me how much Billy loves me and misses me and wanted us to be a family again. He begged me to drop the order and let Billy back in my life. He told me Billy would never hurt me and he just had lost his temper and it all was an accident. An accident? Is that how Billy's sick mind had interpreted this whole thing. Did he think he had accidentally thrown me against the wall? That he accidentally gave me a concussion? That he accidentally had been beating me for the past six years? I wasn't buying it. I felt sorry for him. I desperately wanted to hang on to the Billy who surprised me with a honeymoon in Concord, the Billy who would run a half mile from the other side of campus just to see me for 90 seconds before going to his next class, the Billy who helped old men with flat tires and old ladies with their groceries, the Billy I fell in love with. But that Billy wasn't this Billy. I know it must have been devastating for him to fail the Bar Exam, but what he was doing was devastating me and the kids and I wasn't going to subject myself or my children to any more of this.

He continued to work in the firm as a paralegal, and they allowed him to take the exam again in July. If he failed this time, he would be fired. He was living in New York City near the office with some guy he worked with, so I really wasn't feeling threatened or bothered by him. He would occasionally send me a check, but I never knew when it would come or how much it would be for. I had divorce papers drawn up and of course he refused to sign them. It was almost time for our court appearance on the restraining order. I could either ask for an extension or drop it. I hinted to him that if he agreed to the divorce, I would drop the restraining order and he could see the kids again. He signed the papers in a flash. I only allowed him to see the kids in public places on Sundays. Rico or I would bring them to him in a restaurant or arcade and hang around until it was time for the visit to end. I did not trust him being totally alone with the kids.

Come May, he had to stop the Sunday visitations because he needed to study again for the bar exam. It did not really bother the kids too much. I think Joey was very resentful of his father. He was only five years old when the horror scene happened last winter, but he was very protective of me and saw daddy as an evil monster. It took a lot of restraint, but I never bad-mouthed Billy in front of the kids. I did not want them growing up to think that half of them was bad. Olivia was a bit more forgiving. Little girls have a special bond with their dads. She almost was taking on the role of his caretaker. As much as I praised her for what she did and told her she did exactly the right thing, she may have felt that it was her fault that all the bad things happened to her daddy when she called 911. She felt sorry for him, but also would not allow herself to get too close to him, for fear of being hurt. She was way wise beyond her six years.

Through all this, I was getting very little support from him financially because he was making such a low salary. Thankfully, my business was booming. I think many of my friends knew what was happening and they were recommending me left and right to friends of theirs and I had almost more orders than I knew what to do with. Mary and I worked round the clock filling Easter orders, and I was fortunate enough to have a cool spring season and be able to stay open through Mother's Day. I was concerned about what I would do in the summer when I would have to close and not have any income for three months.

I am a firm believer that prayers do get answered. They may not always be for what we ask for, but they are always for the right thing. Good comes out of even bad situations, so I have learned to trust God and just let Him answer my prayers in the order He sees fit, and also to trust that the way He answers my prayers is exactly the right way for me. I had been praying for a solution to my summer money problem. My prayers were answered when this salesman came in from a small homemade ice cream company from New Hampshire. He said he would install ice cream freezers and supply us with a month's worth of free ice cream if we were willing to try out his product.

This turned into the perfect summer substitute for my chocolate. I put a few tables in the front of the store and continued to sell non-meltable candy like gummies and lollipops. I made a fantastic hot fudge sauce and these gorgeous ice cream sundaes that were drawing huge crowds. June ended up being a month in the black, and I was able to order more of this wonderful ice cream for the rest of the summer. My rep was so pleased with my progress that he offered me the exclusive rights to his product in my area. No one within ten miles would be selling his ice cream.

Word got around about my ice cream, and I was soon doing so well I had to hire a high school girl for the remainder of the summer. Even with the added expenses I was able to pay all my bills and still draw enough of a salary for us to live on. I was too busy to think of the fact that I was raising two little kids alone, running a successful business, and still recovering from the physical and emotional wounds of the bad marriage I just left.

My parents and Rico came up for the kid's belated birthday celebration that I held in the summer. My parents did not seem very impressed with the store or the fact that I was making it on my own. I did, however, also invite Sarah and her family and Father Joe. They did nothing but praise my accomplishments and were very proud of the fact that I had rebounded and was able to land on my feet. They gave me the encouragement I needed to continue even on those days when things got so hard and I was so tired I could barely think straight.

My summer helper, Faith, was a real sweetie. She even did some babysitting for me when I had to run to pick up supplies or the very rare instance when I would maybe go see a movie with one of the Mom's I met from summer camp. She reminded me of myself as a teen. She was working in a chocolate shop, as I did in high school. She loved reading and writing and was off to Iona, a local college in the fall to study journalism. She came from a nice family, but money was tight for them and Faith was very unspoiled and very appreciative of the fact that I let her have flexibility to accommodate her school work, and sent her home with lots of broken chocolate! I could always re-melt the broken stuff, but I knew she had some younger brothers and sisters at home that really looked forward to the treat. Her mom was very good to us. She would have us over for dinner sometimes on a Sunday. It was so nice to be in a family situation again. Her dad was strict but had a heart of gold. He kept his kids in line and they were marvelous because of it. I never heard him raise his voice. He just had a 'look' that would stop them dead in their tracks if they were stepping out of line. Faith adored her father. It almost hurt sometimes for me to see the two of them together knowing Olivia would never have the daily interaction with Billy that Faith is enjoying, and that Billy wasn't stable enough to ever give his little girl the kind of tenderness that Faith's father gave to her.

My own dad was really distant. My mother ruled the roost and he just stayed in the background agreeing to all she said and never making any statements or taking any stands of his own. I love him dearly and he is just a teddy bear, but as far as him ever taking an interest in what I was doing or what I was all about, that was not there. I had always hoped my children would have a better relationship with their father, but I guess it just was not in the cards. One thing is for sure, and the only thing I really can control, they will certainly have a better relationship with me than I had with my mother. I could never hold a grudge against one of my children for as long as she has held it over me. I also do not think, and I pray that I will not be so quick to condemn one of my children for any mistakes in judgment they may make.

Billy was laying low for a while studying, so I felt a calmness. I was not looking forward to the day the July exam would be over. It was the letdown after the February exam that made him go crazy last time. This was even worse since his job was riding on this exam. I did take comfort in the fact that he didn't live with me anymore and so I would not be in the line of fire, but somehow, he had a way of reaching me even without being in the same town as me. I wanted to keep him away from the kids for as long as possible as well, even though I knew he had visitation and I could not deprive him of seeing his children. Unfortunately, you cannot keep a father from seeing his children based on gut instinct. Since he had never done anything to physically harm the kids, he was allowed access to them. He remained at the firm awaiting the results of the July Bar Exam. Hard to believe that a test is taken in July and the results do not post until November! How an educational board can toy with people's lives like that is totally unconscionable.

He saw the kids less and less and did not really seem to care that much anymore. Finally, the results came in November. He had failed again. His firm fired him. He decided the only thing he could do was move back to Boston and try to get a job up there.   I finally felt at peace.

Chris Chapter 22

We finished our last set, which was probably one of the best we ever played. There's just something about a compliment that makes you want to live up to it. The semester was nearly over, and we all had some tests next week, so we decided to make it an early night. As we were leaving to go, I noticed this group of older women probably in their late twenties and thirties who seemed to be out of place here, but very comfortable with each other. They were a tight unit. The kind of group that you notice, but never look at too long because you know they travel in packs and you'd never have a chance of talking to one without the whole pack inspecting you and putting you under the microscope. No guy likes that kind of scrutiny, and women know this, so when they're in a tight group like that you know you should just look the other way, because there's no woman there who is looking for a man. They just want to hang with their girls for a night and be left alone.

One woman had broken away from the pack. Kind of like the lone star on the Texas flag.

I was able to notice her, really notice her without all the others around her. She was confidant, graceful, self-assured but also vulnerable. Something about her was just so enticing. I've dated a lot of girls my age, but I just never could make a connection. They were all kind of vapid and flippy and seldom had a serious thought in their heads. They were all neurotic college girls who were more concerned about how you would look to their friends than who you were, or how you treated them. I found it easier to just not bother. Had a pretty full plate anyway. My schoolwork and my music occupied me almost 24/7. I really didn't need a woman messing up my head.

Since I had just declared to myself that I was going to avoid women, I was a bit surprised to find my feet walking me towards this one, the lone break-away from the pack. I tried to move in another direction, but I was magnetically drawn to her. Before I knew it, I was by her side. In a place like this you really can't smell much more than beer and cigarettes. As I got close to her, I smelt cleanliness. It wasn't a cheap overpowering perfumy smell, she just smelt clean and it rose above the grimy smells of Gary's. I noticed the scent intensified when she tossed her hair back. It was that beautiful silky brown hair of hers that smelt so good. There was also a confidence radiating from her. Maybe she was my clean well-lighted place?

Here I was really close to her, in fact next to her. Me the songwriter, and I couldn't come up with something to say. This was trouble. A woman who could actually make me tongue-tied. I had never had this feeling before. As if she read my mind, she miraculously let me off the hook and spoke first.

"I really enjoyed your music!"

"Well thank you, Ma'am" Oh, hell why did I call her 'Ma'am? Older women get freaked out by that. I didn't want her to think I thought she was some old relic; I just was trying to be polite. I just blew it. Once again as if she sensed what I was thinking she said,

"I love how polite you Texans are."

Whew, maybe I didn't blow it! I would have to be careful now, "So you're not from these parts?" I could already tell from her accent that she wasn't a southerner.

"No, I'm from New Jersey originally. I'm just here for a business conference. I was having dinner with a few of my colleagues. They wanted to leave when they saw what a young crowd it was, but then you guys started playing, and I convinced them to stay."

She was so sweet and had such a great smile. I could just look at her all day and all night long should I be so lucky. "So, did you enjoy our music?" Oh, I'm such a jerk, she just said she enjoyed our music, now I look like I'm either fishing for a compliment, or I wasn't paying attention to her.

Again, she wasn't put off by my obvious lack of social skills. She answered, "Oh, yes, you boys are very talented. But I suppose you hear that all the time..."

"Not more than twice a night." I said with a slight smile still a little giddy over the talk I had with Cy. "Are you at the beginning or end of your trip?"

"This is my last night in Texas. I fly back late tomorrow. That means I have tomorrow to sightsee or relax which is fine with me."

"Well, if you would care to have a genuine Texan show you around the beautiful city of Lubbock, I would be honored." It was again one of those moments when I thought I might have said too much and might have blown it. She's with her posse, what would she want to do with some kid from a cheesy bar? This woman was so fine. I couldn't take my eyes off her and I feared embarrassing myself with each word that fell out of my mouth. "I mean with your colleagues of course"

She smiled a bit and said, "Of course" as if she knew I just had thrown that in to be polite, but I wanted her all to myself and could care less about showing the other women around town. "We didn't make any group plans for tomorrow. Most of the people I'm with are making earlier flights. I would love to see this beautiful town of yours. I came to Texas to live deliberately..."

"…What did you say?" I had to ask in case I didn't hear her right.

"Never mind, sometimes I paraphrase authors," she answered.

"That's Thoreau. He's my favorite. *I went to the woods because I wished to live deliberately, to front only the essential facts of life, and see if I could not learn what it had to teach, and not, when I came to die, discover that I had not lived.*" I knew that quote by heart. I could tell she was impressed. Heck, I even impressed myself with that one.

"Yes, that is exactly the quote I was eluding to! Wow, no one ever gets my little quote paraphrases. You must be very well read." She seemed genuinely excited.

"I'm majoring in English Lit over at Texas Tech. I know what you mean, though. I often feel like people don't get me. When I write songs, I try to put things in simple terms so that I can reach more people. If I really wrote what I was thinking, nobody'd understand it but me."

"So, what's wrong with that? You have to be true to yourself. You can't let other's limitations limit you." She said.

"I never thought of it that way. You are amazing. I can't believe I have totally lost my manners, my name is Chris, and you are…."

"Lucy" She extended her hand to me. "It's so nice to meet you Chris." I took her hand and kissed it in a very gallant cowboy type of gesture. I saw her face change to a shy almost schoolgirl-ish look.

"My pleasure, Lucy. I hope I didn't embarrass you when I said you were amazing, but you gotta understand I only meet college girls who don't have a serious thought in their head. It's really a privilege to talk to someone who knows literature, and who can carry on a conversation."

"I know what you mean. I haven't been single long, but I hesitate getting out there because my single friends tell me men my age only want to talk about themselves and how important their jobs are and how much money they make. A Thoreau quote would be totally lost on them."

I took that to mean she was divorced. I wouldn't pry in case it was a sore subject. I just hoped I could make her feel comfortable enough to open up to me. "I mean it; I would be honored to show you around tomorrow. Do you like Texas BBQ? I know this great joint that has the best in Lubbock."

"I would love it. I'll give you my number. Give me a call in the morning and we can arrange a meeting time."

"That sounds great. I really am glad I bumped into you tonight, Lucy." I took her hand and raised it to my lips to kiss it again. Her hand was so soft and delicate in my big paws. She was like some beautiful, fragile bird and I was trying to be as gentle as I could so as not to scare her and make her fly away. I looked deeply into her soft brown eyes and could feel emotions I never knew I had, start to make themselves known to me. Every part of me wanted to make her a part of me. I just wanted to hold on to this girl and never let go. Not just her body, which was awesome, but her mind, which was even more fabulous. I lingered with my lips pressed gently against the smooth flesh of her hand, just loving the scent still coming from her hair. Man, I could have just died at that moment and say I left this earth a happy man. If I could feel like this just holding her hand.... whoa, I don't even want to think about it!

I was on pins and needles all morning waiting for a good time to call her. I didn't want to call too early, since we did part on the late side last night, and I didn't want to wake her. I didn't want to call too late, because then she would think I forgot or I wasn't interested, and man, was I interested! I thought 10:00 was a good, safe time. I dialed her phone number and held my breath until I heard that angel voice with the slight Jersey accent on the other end. We made our plans and I picked her up at her hotel. I was embarrassed to take her in my old pick-up, but if she wanted to see Lubbock, this was the way to go. I met her in the hotel lobby. When I saw her come down the hallway, I swear I could feel my heart doin' a little Texas two-step in my chest. I hoped she wouldn't notice how goofy she was making me feel. As I helped her into the car, I got a whiff of that hair again. Oh man, this was going to be a great day!

I was trying real hard to live in the here and now and not think about the fact that she would be gone in a few hours. I would just have to savor every minute of the time we had together. Maybe I could see her over the summer. I could get some time off. Maybe she would come back to Lubbock. Maybe I was putting my cart before the horse. We had a fantastic day. We went to some of the prettiest spots in Lubbock and finished off with a good old-fashioned Texas BBQ meal. She loved it. The whole time we talked about books we'd read and philosophy and music, everything! I had never connected with a woman before on so many levels as I did with Lucy. I thought by the time we were in the BBQ place and our mouths were rimmed in red BBQ sauce there was nothing we couldn't do together.

"Lucy, how is it that some city slicker from up north hasn't staked his claim on you?"

"Well, Chris, I'm technically still married, I'm separated. I just got out of an abusive marriage" Man, I thought that illegal chop block to the knee hurt? That weren't nothing compared to this. This was a chop block straight to my heart. How could anyone ever hurt this sweet angel? She must have noticed that the wind was completely out of my sails, because she continued. "I'll be divorced soon. I'm not a quitter, I really tried to make it work for the sake of my kids, but I was in a losing battle.

I didn't know quite how to respond to that kind of revelation. She's still married. I'm stompin on some other guy's turf. Did she say kids? I didn't want her to think that the fact that she had kids freaked me out. Heck, maybe it did! "It must be very hard for you." That was about the best I could come up with.

"It is extremely hard. When I first met him, he was very different. Now he's turned into a big bully. I just wanted him out of my life."

"He doesn't…still hurt you, does he? Cause if he does, I'd have to show him why Texan's wear boots!"

"Chris, you are so very sweet, you remind me of my big brother. No, since we separated, he's just all talk. He's got a medical condition called bipolar disorder. It hurts that I can't help him, but I can't help him and be safe at the same time. I hope I haven't laid too much on you."

"No, No of course not. Heck, I appreciate your honesty. Anyway, what can a guy like me hope for except friendship from a smart, sexy, funny woman like you?"

"You will definitely get friendship. That's a given. I have had such a great time today with you. I feel reborn, and like there is still some life left in me. Billy didn't take it all away. Thanks for showing me that."

"I don't know what this guy did, but he was a fool to ever cause you a minute of unhappiness. Some guys just don't know what they've got." I confess, I may have tried to go a little over the line with Lucy, I just couldn't resist her, but she pulled me back to the reality of the situation, and I decided right then and there that she was worth waiting for, and eventually our day would come.

Lucy and I spent as much time as we could together before her flight.

We laid the foundation for a great friendship and perhaps the fact that she was married threw me a bit. I'm just a dumb college guy. What did I know about abusive husbands and divorce and kids? It was a like a whole new passel of material to write songs about, but I felt like I would be exploiting my friendship with Lucy if I did that. It did give me some insight into a different world that I was never real privy to. I guess this was what Cy meant by getting some mud on my wheels. Lucy was my clean well-lighted place, but she was my mud too.

I might have been getting in over my head, but damn the water felt good! I wanted to be intimate with her the worst way, but I knew if I did, it could have just been over in a day and I might never see her again. I thought if I didn't scare her off, maybe we could actually build something. We started a friendship that would last a lifetime. After she left, we called each other almost every day. There wasn't a day that went by when I didn't ask myself why I let her go.

Lucy Chapter 23

There was going to be a large chocolate convention in Lubbock Texas of all places, and I was toying with the idea of going. It would just be a long weekend, and I could use the interaction with other chocolatiers to maybe get some fresh ideas. A change of scenery after all the ugliness of the past year might be just what I needed. Rico insisted on staying with the kids and they were so excited about having a weekend with 'Uncle Good-time' that I could not say no. Mary and Faith agreed to mind the shop so off I was to Lubbock. The seminars were fascinating, and I found many new vendors for boxes, and other supplies. The trip had been well worth my time. After the first day I met a few other women who had chocolate shops in different parts of the country. We swapped some war stories and had dinner together. One of the ladies who was a bit older than me, but quite put together suggested that we check out the local nightlife in Lubbock. I was going to beg off and go back to my room, but then I heard Rico's voice in my ear telling me to go out and have fun. I decided a few hours couldn't hurt, so we went to this little dive looking bar in an out of the way corner of town. We immediately felt a bit out of place because we realized that the college age crowd was much younger than us. We were all set to leave when the band started playing and I heard this singer begin singing. He was awesome. I had to stay to hear more and convinced my new friends to do the same.

After the first set I spotted the lead singer who was about 20 years old. He was built like my brother but had a more preppy-cowboy look. I had not approached a guy since the day I met Billy, and I hoped he wouldn't take this as a come-on, but I had to tell him how his music touched me. His name was Chris Steele, and he was a student at Texas Tech. He had such a gentle way about him, I felt instantly comfortable. He offered to give me a tour of Lubbock the following day and to my surprise I found myself accepting.

What a sweet kid! He was such a Texas gentleman. He had a charming way about him. I felt like a teenager when he kissed my hand, or helped me into his truck, or the way he looked at me, like I was the most beautiful woman alive. I even noticed that when we stood close together, he would bend forward a bit to inhale the smell of my hair. He was so good for my damaged ego. I felt alive again, and safe. I also felt very comfortable around him. We went to this Texas barbeque place for ribs and I told him about my failed marriage. I promised myself I wouldn't be one of those woman who blurts out to everyone she meets about what a hard life she's had, but there was something so wise and reassuring about Chris that I couldn't help telling him everything.

I was ashamed of my feelings. After all he was just a college kid, and I was 8 years older than he was. And worse, I was still married to Billy, technically. I should not have allowed myself to have those kind of feelings for him, but he made it very difficult for me not to trust him and like him…a lot.

We talked about everything and eventually got to my favorite subject, literature and Thoreau. We shared quotes we liked. The first Thoreau quote I put out there was,

"The mass of men lead lives of quiet desperation."

I found it a bit difficult to articulate why I picked this quote, but after I said it Chris lit up.

"That's one of my favorite quotes, too," he said.

There was something in his eyes that spoke volumes to me. He went on to say "Most men are desperate. They are desperate for love, desperate for fulfillment, desperate for validation, for excitement, adventure. But they remain silent and do nothing about it." I was focusing intently on his words and the sound of his soothing southern drawl. He continued, "They quietly live their lives with these unfulfilled needs and desires swirling about them feeling as though they are sinking deeper and deeper into this desperate hole, and just screaming silently to be rescued, or to have someone help them out of the hole."

"Screaming silently?" I asked. That seemed like an interesting concept and I wanted to know what he meant, because I have been having similar thoughts myself, I just was never able to express them as eloquently as he just did.

"Yes," he answered, "it's when you are burning with a longing to do something or have a hidden desire, but for the sake of propriety and to appear as though you fit in with the masses, you keep it within you, knowing that the silent screaming will keep you up nights, invade your every free moment, and haunt you until you finally must answer the screams and do whatever it is that you are longing to do."

"Do you mean only physical desires?" I asked wondering exactly what level he was speaking on.

"No" He shook his head and had the slightest playful glint in his eyes. "The desires can be to break out from a situation like a bad marriage, or a dead end job, or to fulfill a lifelong dream like jumping out of an airplane, or doing something simply because it is what you want to do, not what someone says you must do." He was so passionate when he spoke and had such a way of delivering his message. I had to keep reminding myself that he was only twenty years old. He spoke with such authority, maturity and persuasiveness. Passion was the emotion he was bringing out in me. "Those are the things that we quietly keep inside, that make us one of the masses, but cause our desperation. Thoreau felt we truly find ourselves through nature and wildness, and I feel that way too. Like the opposite of quiet desperation is wildness." He paused for a moment, took a swig of beer from a long-neck bottle, then looked at me as if no one else were around and asked, "So why did you pick that quote?"

I was so totally entrenched in his explanation that whatever my reason was for feeling that quote spoke to me, I had completely forgotten. "Do you mind if we stay a little longer so we can discuss that quote? I think there was more to you choosing it than you are admitting to." I noticed that in that booth in a very dark corner it felt like we were the only ones in that crowded BBQ place that suddenly felt very cozy and intimate.

"What do you mean?" It irked me that he was able to see right through me, but in a way, I was flattered.

"Just mean that I think you may be suppressing some silent screams yourself, and maybe you might want to talk about it with someone. I'm not trying to come on to you, I just see a kind of faraway look in your eyes."

Chris was leaning in towards me looking very innocent, but sexy as all hell. I knew I should not have said this, but I did, "Sure, I would like to finish our conversation."

I probably should have known just by the fact that he said he wasn't trying to come on to me that he was. Men don't usually make such a disclaimer unless that is exactly what is on their minds. I guess there was a part of me that was so lonely and desperate that I needed a bit of a diversion in my life. There was also a big part of me that was rather naïve and did hope we could continue the conversation. I was away from home and from Billy and the torment he put me through. I knew our dead marriage was never all I had dreamed marriage would be, but until this very moment I had never given a thought to filling my lonely hours with another man.

He reached closer to the table so he could rest his bottle, then he gently reached for my hands and held them in his big soft hands. I was going to pull away, but I felt so comfortable in his presence and his hands were so warm and reassuring.

"I think you are silencing your screams. You have such a sad, and lonely look in your eyes. I can tell by much of what you've told me tonight that you are leading a life of quiet desperation. You picked that quote for a very good reason. You recognize that you are just one of the masses of 'men' in a desperate situation, yearning to break free. You are the proverbial bird with a broken wing. You haven't been allowed to fly or to sing, and I bet you want to."

As he spoke, I could not stop looking at him. He wasn't classically good looking, but had an undeniable charisma and just such a way about him that you thought he was more and more handsome as you got to know him and see his heart. He was over six feet tall with wavy dark hair that was neatly trimmed but fell sort of youthfully down his forehead. He had a fantastic body and these deep blue eyes that melted me. I had forgotten how to act around guys. He was also smart and intuitive and sensitive, and the more we talked the more drawn into him I was. I guess I had shut the sexual side of me off since Billy was so far off the deep end, and I was just too down on myself and this life I was living to think about being attractive to men anymore. I was totally thrown off guard by this whole night and wasn't quite sure what I wanted to do about it.

"Are you okay? Maybe we should have another drink?" He suggested. That sounded like an excellent idea. He ordered another beer and ordered me a glass of white zinfandel. I knew right then and there he must have liked me, if a Texan was not embarrassed to order a glass of white zinfandel. I wished at that moment that I could have tolerated whiskey or tequila, but I'm not much of a drinker, so I had to hope this would pack enough of a punch because I needed to feel the effects of alcohol as soon as possible. I needed to blur my rational thoughts so I could justify the irrational thing I was contemplating doing. We chatted a bit more about deep thoughts, all the time he was subtly and almost unnoticeably moving closer to me in the booth. I could smell his cologne. It was masculine and woodsy. So woodsy it reminded me vaguely of Christmas. My mind drifted to my first Christmas with Billy and how happy we once were. Guilt crept in to spoil the mood Chris had so masterfully created.

I drifted back into the moment when I realized my glass was empty and his beer was nearing the bottom as well. "More wine?" he asked.

"Sure." I knew I shouldn't have said yes but wasn't able to make a rational decision in that moment. Then he looked me straight in the eye, something Billy never did, and said "Lucy, I will never hurt you." He leaned forward and started to kiss me. His lips were so soft and warm. He cradled the back of my head in his big soft hands and for what seemed like four days I got lost in his kiss. Of course, in reality it was just a few moments, but it just seemed as if time stopped while his lips were touching mine.

Because I had more wine, I could blame the alcohol for my lack of control. I started to kiss him back. There is a point in every kiss when you are the kisser or the kissee. I started off as the kissee, but I became the kisser. I leaned into him and took over. I did what I had been dying to do all night; I ran my fingers through his thick, wavy hair. I could taste the beer on his breath or now was it on mine? It was hard to tell and I didn't care. This felt so good, to be feeling passion again.

Then, reality set in. I could feel his hand under the table moving ever so carefully up my leg under my sundress. I knew where this was going and part of me wanted nothing more than to leave there with him and for him to just have me, have all of me, and make me feel alive again for a night.

I needed to silence the screams that had been residing in my head for so long. But I couldn't. I had a plane to catch.

I sat up straight and stopped kissing him. I moved his hand away and felt the burning in my eyes from unfallen tears and the lump developing in my throat. I told him I couldn't go further. I couldn't get involved with someone while technically I still had a husband. I wasn't raised that way and I didn't feel good about it.

He took my hand again and kissed it and said, "I'm sorry, I didn't mean to make you feel uncomfortable. You are a good person, and I that is one of the reasons why I am so drawn to you. I wouldn't want you to do anything you would regret. I really like you, and I am truly sorry if I crossed a line. I guess we should go now."

A part of me wanted to stay. A part of me wanted to finish that second glass of wine and forget that the last five minutes ever happened and go back to the magic of that kiss. And a part of me wanted to just put myself before a quarry full of good and righteous people armed with stones for what I had contemplated doing. Instead I just thanked him for being so understanding, reassured him that if the circumstances were different, I would not have been able to resist him, and thanked him for making me feel good about myself again.

"You should feel good about yourself. You are a beautiful, amazing woman with a great deal to offer, and your husband was one stupid man!"

He kissed my hand again as we got up to go and said, "Please don't let this mean we can't be friends. I never met anyone who I can talk to the way I can talk to you."

"I'm not going anywhere. Of course we can be friends." He gave me a wink. I felt I had made the right choice. When the end of the day came

138

and he drove me to the airport, I was incredibly tired, incredibly happy to be going back to my kids, and incredibly sad to be leaving this new special friend.

Billy Chapter 24

That whiny bitch must have said something to her psycho brother because I was in my apartment minding my own business when I hear this motorcycle pull up and then a pounding on my door. I knew I shouldn't have opened it, but my car was out front so he would have known I was there and broken the door down. Besides, I'm a lawyer. I can talk this simpleton out of whatever he came here to do. He's not that bright.

Before he was barely in the door, he grabbed the collar of my shirt and lifted me off the floor with it, so I was staring right into his cold brown eyes. "What did you do to my sister?" He demanded.

My heart was pounding. Rico's a very big guy and pretty scary looking. I tried to act composed and not let him smell my fear. I figured my best way out of this was to lie. "It was an accident; she tripped and fell. What did she tell you?"

"Enough for me to know it wasn't no accident and it wasn't the first time." He shook me hard and then dropped me. I fell to the floor with a hard thud. Then he kicked me in the groin with his hard leather boot and said this is just a warning. Me and my buddies will be coming next if I ever hear you lay a hand on her. The only reason I'm letting you live is because I don't want to hurt those kids. But I swear, if you fuckin go near Lucy again, they will never find your body."

Then I got stupid and said "Get out or I'll call the police"

He picked me up again with a new round of hate in his eyes and yelled, "You'll call the police you fuckin wife beater? Go ahead. There ain't a cop in town who's gonna go against the club. You want a little extra punishment? The cops would be a good place to start. Where's your phone, I'll dial 911 for you" I knew he was right. The cops give the riders a lot of respect and I would be making a big mistake by pissing them off too.

"Ok, ok, what do you want me to do?"

"Disappear, let her get on with her life. Don't call her, harass her or threaten her in any way. As far as the kids go, you only see them if I'm around. You got that?"

"Yes" Finally he put me down. He slammed the door on his way out and I started to shake and cry. Suddenly, I was that fourth grader on the bus again.

I knew I had to do something drastic if I was ever to see my kids and Lucy again. I loved her. I loved my kids. I'm not a bad person, I just don't know what comes over me sometimes. I feel like two different people. I feel trapped by this other horrible side of me that takes over and does stupid thing just to ruin my life. I need to get help and get it fast. I decided that the only way I was ever going to win Lucy back was to control this other side of me. There must be doctors who know what to do with someone like me.

Without giving away that I was asking for myself, I got the name of a good psychiatrist from the social worker at the DA's office. I was diagnosed as having bipolar disorder. There was something chemically out of whack in my system which made me turn into a monster. Lucy always said she knew when I was about to blow up because my skin changed color and I had a different smell about me. I used to get furious when she said that, but now, I see she was just much more perceptive about those things than I was. I took some vacation time so I could get regulated on the medication. I went to intensive therapy everyday as an outpatient in a psychiatric hospital until I was finally deemed under control. The doctors said I would never be perfect, but I would be much more in control of my emotions and now that I know the signs that an episode is coming I would be better able to remove myself from the situation before I blew my stack. This was all progress, and I was anxious to share all this with Lucy.

I had much to overcome. I was asking her to forget a lot and start fresh with me. It wasn't going to be easy to convince her that I had changed, and I wouldn't blame her for being skeptical. I had my work cut out for me, but I had to have her back in my life. She deserved the best life possible and I was determined to give it to her.

Diana Chapter 25

Having Rico in my life has changed everything. I wake up happy, I go to bed happy. I eat, like a real person. I feel like a real person. More importantly, I am finally beginning to see outside myself and what my illness was doing to everyone around me. I really hurt my mother and for that I am truly sorry. I treated her to a trip to Concord this summer. I hoped it would heal her the way it healed me. She's been so down since dad died. She was such a vibrant, interesting woman. I wanted her to get some of her old spark back. She just retired from teaching and needs some new focus in her life. She moved to New York and helps Rico's sister at her chocolate shop. They formed a friendship when she worked at a candy shop on the Shore and mom was a customer. It's a good start, but maybe the magical waters of Walden Pond will heal her like they healed me.

Chris Chapter 26

"Simplify, Simplify." Henry David Thoreau

Early on I wrote a song for Lucy called Quiet Desperation. It was based on the Thoreau quote that goes: *"The mass of men lead lives of quiet desperation."* This was always our quote.

Silent screams,
Quiet desperation.
Nothing seems
To end the conversation
Going on
In my mind,
Can't find the inspiration.
Only you
Can put an end to
My quiet desperation.

When our souls connected
I was too young to know
You would live in every thought
Haunting my heart so.
I couldn't see another
Couldn't feel or eat or breathe
Without your soul
Right there with mine
Residing only in my dreams.

Silent screams,
Quiet desperation
Nothing seems
To end the conversation

Going on
In my mind,
Can't find the inspiration.
Only you
Can put an end to
My quiet desperation.

I was screaming oh so silently
My soul begging that you'd hear,
But hoping that you couldn't tell
How much of you I feared
How could I touch my angel?
Would it mean my life would end?
Or would holding you
Be the start,
Of life with my best friend?

Silent screams,
Quiet desperation.
Nothing seems
To end the conversation
Going on
In my mind,
Can't find the inspiration.
Only you
Can put an end to
My quiet desperation.

It became my signature song and blew the Lubbock Desperados off the charts professionally. We were the hottest ticket in town. It's about the silent screaming that goes on in my head. Most people are screaming silently because they want to fit in and be part of the masses. They don't and can't satisfy their desires or follow their heart because doing so may make them stand out from the crowd, so in order to blend in they silently scream, and lead lives of quiet desperation. For me, I was screaming silently because of fear. I had two incredible choices in front of me. One was to keep going with my career, living like a gypsy, making obscene money and being famous. The other choice was to live a quiet happy life with the woman I love and just be a regular guy. Neither was a bad choice; I just chose the wrong door. It's funny how a song about what I can't have, brought me everything I didn't need.

In choosing music I lead a life of quiet desperation and am kept up nights by the silent screams in my head. Lucy was the answer to my silent screaming.

We met up as often as we could after she was divorced, and we had this unearthly relationship. We had amazing conversations. We could see into each other's souls. It was magic every time I was with her and I wished it could last forever. Or did I? I never had these feelings for any woman before, and I was afraid of what I felt. I knew if I stayed with her, I would have to marry her. There would be no other option, so I did something that I regret every day of my life...I ran. Each and every time, I went back to Nashville under the poor guise that I had to be there for the band. If I really wanted to, I could have stayed with her, and if I had the courage, I could have asked her to come along with me. I never did ask because I was always afraid of what her answer would be.

I didn't have the courage. It bothered me that I was a hypocrite. My songs are all about being honorable, standing up to your fears, standing tall and not running away. So, what did I do? I ran away from the one thing that can never hurt you, only make you stronger...love.

Through the years I thought about her constantly. I saw her everywhere I went. Every brunette woman with shoulder length hair would be her...until they turned their face towards me. I had lots of woman share

146

a bed with me during my years on the road, but nothing came near the relationship I had with Lucy. We were Soulmates. We had a special bond and in my mind we still do. Every time I am out with some model or actress at some function or award show I wish it were Lucy on my arm instead. I tried to dilute my unhappiness by immersing myself in my career. In music that is very easy to do.

The next few years were out of control. I couldn't believe how quickly my career took off, and now it was on fire. Cy was right. I was able to write with more edge after having met Lucy. I knew what love was and I knew what it wasn't. I knew what it felt like to want something you couldn't have, and to have something you couldn't want. I had all this fame, and I was making a ton of money. The Lubbock Desperados first CD was certified platinum and me and Clay and Ronnie were riding high. We were touring the country on our first big city tour. We were a part of the George Strait Country Music Fest, which is a huge accomplishment for a young band. We had all moved up to Nashville and I was writing not just for myself, but for other stars to record as well. I was getting known as the best singer-songwriter currently on Music Row.

Lucy remained my friend, but at the same time I was so busy I knew I couldn't offer her much of a relationship. Me and the band were on such a whirlwind ride that I didn't think it was fair to suck anyone else into this twister. I decided it was best we remain friends and keep it at that. We would see each other when the band toured New York, or sometimes I would send her tickets to fly to a concert we were giving in another city. Every time I was with her I thought about chucking this whole crazy life I was living and just stay with her, but then I would look at my schedule and see I was booked solid clear into the next two years. I couldn't disappoint all the people who bought tickets to my concerts or those whose livelihoods depended on the Desperados being on the road. I was too busy to start any kind of relationship, and Lucy deserved more than that. It was my immense love for her that kept me away from her. I

147

knew I was playing a dangerous game and that I could risk losing her to someone else forever, but in the back of my mind I thought maybe I didn't deserve her since I couldn't give her 100% of me. It wouldn't have been fair of me to ask her to share me with my career.

5 years after we met in Lubbock, I sent tickets for her and the kids to join me in Disney World for a TV special I was shooting. I got them hooked up VIP all the way. The kids were 13 and 14 and they had a blast. Lucy and I had a few moments together, but my schedule kept us from really connecting. It finally hit me that in spite of the fact that I could buy her anything she desired, I had nothing to offer her. Lucy didn't care about material things. I think she carried the same purse she had the night I met her in Lubbock, even though I send her designer bags all the time. I think she donates them to charity. She was so different from all the women I meet on the road. All she wanted from me was the one thing I couldn't give her, my time. I thought it was best to do what I always did, walk, no run away.

We finally had a brief moment together at the park with the fireworks going off above us, so cliché, but so damn pretty.

"Darlin', I just want to tell you how special this time has been with you and your kids. I wish it could have been more alone time without my job getting in the way."

"Chris, I know you have obligations and everybody wants a piece of you, but I can't help miss that guy I met 5 years ago so wise beyond his years, so thoughtful, so sensitive. I can't help but think about what it might be like if we were together."

"I think about it too, all the time. I can't take you along on this circus I live in. Not after what you went through with Billy. I would never hurt you like that; you know that. I'm just afraid I would hurt your heart

148

which would be even worse." I pulled a little away from her because I didn't want to feel the chill from the cold words I was about to throw on her. "I think we should just stay friends and never think this can be any more than that."

I saw the bright flecks in her brown eyes go dim and those perfect little lips puffed out ever so slightly. She just stayed there for a moment and didn't say a word. It was the longest moment I had ever lived through. Then she spoke.

"I understand. You're a celebrity, I'm just a chocolate maker from New Jersey. I always feel like the princess in that castle over there when I am with you." She pointed to the iconic Cinderella's castle, "but I know I can't have you. It's just been a fantasy that I've allowed myself to indulge in."

"Honey, you deserve that castle, and that mountain, and that spaceship," I said pointing at the landmarks in this Magic Kingdom. "and I want you to find the man who will give it all to you, I just know that right now, it's not me. You'll meet someone amazing who will be there for you and not just give you 5 minutes before a show. I want that for you." She was nodding in agreement, but the tears clouding her eyes said she did not agree.

"Chris, I guess we had to have this talk eventually. I knew it was coming, but that doesn't make it any easier. I will absolutely not accept you not being in my life. You are still my best friend and that will never change."

We hugged and watched the end of the firework show. The kids were coming off a ride, so we took them for a bite to eat. For a few more moments I could play out my fantasy of being a real family with Lucy. In spite of what I said, I wanted it more than anything. I just couldn't trust that after a few years of living with me and putting up with my crazy life that she would still love me, and that would kill me, and hurt her.

After Disney, things continued to skyrocket for me and the band. I was even getting too busy to write the way I wanted to. Back in the hungry days I used to spend days or weeks working on a song, perfecting it, nurturing it until I thought it was excellent. Instead I was banging them out in a matter of hours and getting huge praise for work that I personally found inferior. There was so much pressure on me to produce. I found myself writing to please the masses instead of pleasing myself. I remember Lucy's words the night we met. She said I shouldn't let other's limitations limit me, but that was exactly what I was doing.

With each CD that was released we made more and more money. The kind of money I never thought I'd see in a lifetime. I was buying cars and homes and all kinds of stuff. It's funny, though, as each CD came out, I was less satisfied with my work, but each CD topped the last in sales. I told Cy about my misgivings and he said it didn't matter what kind of crap I turned out. People loved me and would keep buying me, so just keep it coming.

The celebrity thing gets real old. Everywhere I went people recognized me and wanted to talk to me. Don't get me wrong, I love the fans and always try to stop and say 'hey' or sign something, but I was beginning to feel like I needed a little downtime. I couldn't remember the last time I read a book or even had a deep thought. I was becoming so money focused that nothing else seemed to matter except producing the next big song. There were movie soundtracks, duets, concert tours, award shows, Fan Fair, talk shows, charity benefits, autograph sessions and Christmas albums. It was completely overwhelming. We'd been at this for over 10 years and we had made more money than we knew what to do with. It reached the point where we didn't even have the time to enjoy the money we made or the things it bought us.

I was back in Lubbock at my folk's house one rare night. We were playing this big gig in Lubbock for the benefit of some local charities and I got to spend some time with my Daddy and Momma. We were sitting on the front porch drinking lemonade on a night when everything under the star filled sky seemed to be sighing with relief that the scorching hot Texas sun had set. Daddy went inside to bed leaving me and my mom alone on the porch. We sat there just a rockin' away with the only sounds being our chairs going back and forth on the squeaky floor of the porch and the crickets chirping away. I made a mental note to have a contractor come over and build them a new porch. I've bought them houses all over the country, but they still love our old house, and I'm glad they kept it. It gives me a grounded feeling knowing I will always be able to come home. Finally, my mom broke the silence and said, "Chris, you have become so successful, but my baby boy, I worry about you. Are you happy?"

"What do you mean Momma? I have everything I've ever dreamed of, why wouldn't I be happy?" It's kind of scary the way mommas can see right through us. It's also scary how at age 30 I was still her baby boy.

"Because I remember you telling me you wanted to live the kind of life Henry David Thoreau advocated. You wanted to always work for the love of it, not for money. Sweetheart, do you still love songwriting?"

My momma was such a smart woman, and she knew me like a book. There would be no point in lying to her. "No Momma, I don't love it anymore, in fact I'm beginning to hate it. I feel like I have to dumb down all my lyrics just so they will have wide appeal. I feel disconnected. I feel lost, like I have no ideals or goals anymore. I've achieved all my goals…now what? I sacrificed living a normal life for fame. I started off doing this to share my songs with other people and hopefully inspire them. I haven't written anything in years that I can say I'm proud of. I really need some focus I don't even know what I stand for anymore."

"Honey, I think it's time you rediscover who you are. Back in college your happiest days were when you were studying literature, and your best work as far as I was concerned, was some of the work you did while in school. It was philosophical and meaningful. You never even recorded half of it. That was the real Chris Steele. That was your authentic self. Maybe it's time to reconnect with that guy again."

I could feel a lump forming in my throat and almost was embarrassed to admit this to her, but I always could tell my mom anything. "I don't know how to find him Momma…"

"Go to where it all started for you…go to Walden. Re-read it. You might find some answers there."

I let her words permeate my thick skull. My momma was right. I needed to go to Walden. I decided that not only would I re-read it; I would actually go to Walden. I called my travel agent and had her book a trip for me to go up to Concord, Mass. I would stop in and visit David Henry, my old college creative writing professor who lived up there. He started me on my love of literature and writing; maybe he could help me find it again. My travel agent made plans for me to go there right after the fourth of July. She said there was a gathering of the Thoreau Society the 2nd weekend in July, and the town gets real crowded so if I wanted a peaceful visit I should go before then. She arranged for me to fly into Boston and have a limo take me to this very quaint bed and breakfast where I had the Henry David Thoreau suite. I went up alone. I toyed with the idea of calling on Lucy to join me, but I needed to heal myself first. I was in no condition to offer her anything but a broken man with no real idea of who he was. She deserved more than that, and until I was ready to give her more, I didn't want to keep her from living life.

It was probably the first time I'd been alone in ten years. I never went anywhere without Clay and Ronnie. I love those guys like brothers, but if

I was going to find myself, I had to be by myself. They understood I needed to do this, and I went with their blessing.

I looked up David Henry and asked him if I could come by for a visit. I heard he went blind after I had him as a teacher. I can't imagine anything worse than that. Losing your sight, your ability to see all the beauty of God's green earth. That must be the worst kind of hell.

I got into Concord Thursday afternoon. I was going to spend a few days just being by myself and soaking in as much about this place as I could before I met with David. This place was awesome. I spent a great deal of time in the Thoreau institute reading as much as I could by Thoreau and other Transcendental writers. The thing with Transcendentalists is nature takes the front stage. Once you get back to nature, and you simplify your life, you start getting answers.

"Not till we are lost, in other words, not till we have lost the world, do we begin to find ourselves, and realize where we are and the infinite extent of our relations."
Henry David Thoreau

I drove out to Walden Pond and was amazed at how beautiful it was. There were plants and ferns and things I never saw in any of the places we toured, not that we were ever in one place long enough to take in the natural surroundings anyway. Our closest encounters with nature occurred when the bus might be flying down some country highway and we could see whatever was in season growing out our windows. Some of the musicians might start to reminisce about their childhoods on their daddies' farms and the memories of picking the very crops we were blowing right by. Life on the road is very tough and lonely.

I sat and thought with this beautiful pond here before me. I remembered when I first read Walden and I thought the way he described the pond reminded me of home. It still does. I needed to put the pieces of my life

153

in order. I needed to simplify and simplify is what I would do. It was time to take a little break from the Desperados and find out who I was. Maybe I could do some charity work or spend some time with Lucy. Anytime I saw her it was with one hand on my bag and one foot out the door. I never got to really kick back with her. I haven't been on a long, meaningful date with Lucy or anyone else for that matter since the night I took her out for Texas BBQ. So, let's revisit this…my love life consisted of very brief encounters on the road with groupies, and the memory of ribs with an older woman about 10 years ago. Okay, my life was genuine, certified pathetic. I wanted to settle down one day. I wanted a wife and kids and a home and a dog. I wanted what my parents had. I wanted a quiet, peaceful life with lemonade and rocking chairs on a squeaky front porch. I wondered if any of that was possible. Ironically, it was Thoreau who said,

"The opportunities of living are diminished in proportion as what are called the 'means' are increased."

That boy had the right idea. With every dollar I added to my bank account I felt as if another minute of my life was being deducted.

I wanted to write the kind of songs I used to write when we were singing every Saturday night at Gary's. Those were my favorite songs. I could do it again; I just had to take my time. I took out my cell phone and called Cy. He was a bit perturbed at me because I was supposed to be meeting with the Levi people about promoting their blue jeans but blew it off to come here. At this moment I don't need another commercial deal, I needed to decommercialize. That was it. Everything we did since hitting the big time was so glitzy and commercialized. I needed to unplug. Maybe I should literally unplug and do an acoustic album featuring all new songs written for me, by me. Maybe throw in some acoustic versions of the songs I wrote in college. Cy needed to hear this.

"Hey Cy."

"Hey yourself, where the hell are you? The travel agent said you were going to the woods or something…can't you go a-hunting and a-fishing right here in Tennessee? I need you here, boy. I had to pitch to the Levi people all by myself. They didn't want to see fat old me, they wanted to see your cute ass and how it would look in their jeans."

"Sorry, Cy, I really had to get away. I'm not feeling good about my writing these days. My last CD had a song about rocks falling in love!"

"Hey, 'Stone Love' was number one on Billboard for four weeks. What are you complaining about? Com'on Chris, we've had this talk before. The people love you; does it really matter if it's not the kind of work you love doin'? You're making tons of money off it; you employ sixty people in your entourage. The Desperados are a big business. I don't see what the problem is."

"I've been thinking, Cy, I want to release an all acoustic album with some new songs and some never before released old songs from my college days."

"New songs, did I hear you say new songs? You're writing while you're in the woods! Good boy I knew you wouldn't let me down."

"I'm writing, but I'm writing different. It's the way I was meant to write. You'll see when I get back."

"Good, we'll get working on the new album immediately, I'll get the musicians to start committing to a date in late July.."

"Hold your horses, Cy, didn't you hear what I said? It's going to be an acoustic album. I even have a name for it, actually, my momma came up with it...The Real Chris Steele."

"Chris, acoustic albums never sell. You'd be committing professional suicide."

"It don't really matter to me, Cy. If I'm going to stay in this business, I'm going to do it my way."

"And Clay and Ronnie? How do they fit into this plan? Or are you dumping them? You goin' solo for good?"

"I would never dump my friends; they've got to understand I have to do this. It's this, or I leave music forever."

"Easy now, boy, don't act hasty...okay, when you come back, we'll sit down and see what you've got."

"Thanks, Cy." I clicked off the cell phone and could almost imagine the sweat forming on Cy's wrinkled brow when he thought I might quit music. I knew that was my ace in the hole. He still needed me to be the front man, because there are a lot of people on the Desperados payroll, himself included. It was in his best interest to see that I stay in this business. When I retire, so does he. I wasn't trying to hurt nobody; I just kept hearing the words of Thoreau himself saying;

"Do not hire a man who does your work for money, but him who does it for love of it."

I was just trying to get the love of it back again.

I spent a day with David Henry right before I left Concord. He is some kind of man. He dealt with his blindness and became a critically acclaimed author. He wasn't a best seller, and his work may not be appealing to the masses, but he'll go down in history as one of our

156

greatest writers, I'm sure of it. He never sold out. He sure could have been making a fortune writing Romance novels, but that ain't where it's at for him. He lives a simple life, but one that pleases him. I've never known a man with such a positive and upbeat attitude. He's such a likeable guy too. I asked him why he never married since that question seemed to be weighing heavy on my own mind lately. He said he was deeply in love once with a girl named Mary. His family had to move away, and she moved on. He knew he would never find another who he would love as much as Mary or have that kind of connection with. He chose to marry Mary in his mind, and that would have to be enough for him. Was that what I was doing with Lucy? Was she the only woman for me? Did I make a huge mistake in leaving her to have my career and life on the road? I wondered if it was too late for us, if I could ever find the courage to ask her to be my wife. I was learning a great deal once again from David.

We talked about transcendentalism and nature and simplifying your life. We talked about being true to yourself and not letting the pursuit of money come before the pursuit of self-improvement or doing something you love. We talked about the need for quiet time and how we can't hear the answers if we are never in silence. And we talked about being true to yourself and your calling and doing things that pleased you, and writing not for the masses, but for yourself. After I left him, I wrote 3 new songs.

I went to the woods
Looking for a missing piece of me.
I went to the woods
To see what was right in front of me.
To get back to what is real
To see if I could still feel
I went to the woods.

I lived inside a moment
Carved out just for me.
Like the home a beast had made inside
This storm downed old pine tree.
Sheltered from the troubles
The world around it brings
Filled with nothing more than
The most essential things.
I went to the woods.

I went to the pond
To have the water heal me.
I went to the pond
To see what it would reveal to me.
To wash away my pain
Like a soft New England rain.
I went to the pond.

I walked amid the trees
Until I saw the simple blue
Of a pond so clear and peaceful
I could almost see right through
To the reflection of the heavens
Bouncing on its mirrored face.
Reminding me that this life should be
A walk and not a race.
I went to the pond

In just one day with him I began to see how important it is to pay attention to all your senses. He was so in tune with his sense of smell, and taste, and hearing and touch. He didn't need to rely on sight. He 'saw' all he needed to see with his other senses. Maybe even more so. Sometimes we just speed on by things because we 'see' them. He would stop and take his time discovering other things about them besides what they looked like. I was much more in tune with my other senses when I was younger. I remember the night I met Lucy and how captivated I was by the scent of her hair, the sound of her voice, the feel of her presence near me, and the taste of her skin when I kissed her hand.

Mary Chapter 27

"The only danger in Friendship is that it will end." Henry David Thoreau.

When I arrived in Concord Thursday, late morning, the second week of July, I was at once feeling relief that my trip ended, and excitement that I had fulfilled a life-long dream to come here. I was trying to do things like this since my husband passed away. My children kept telling me that it was time I start to live again. I found this very easy for them to say, but very difficult for me to implement.

I almost lost my daughter. She was anorexic. I always felt personally guilty about this. I am not sure what I could have done to have triggered this in her. I never focused on weight...she never was overweight. She always had the opinion of herself that she was fat and there was nothing I or Arthur or anyone could ever say that would make her feel any different. She reached rock bottom but met a wonderful guy who totally transformed her back into the confident daughter I once had. Her hero might not look exactly like a typical hero, but in my book, he is Superman, and I am forever grateful to Rico for giving me back my Diana.

Part of her transformation took place on a trip to Walden Pond in Concord which is why she was so adamant about me coming up here now that I have gone through such a rough spot after losing my dear Arthur.

I have been trying to do things to take my mind off losing Arthur, to rekindle some old hobbies and interests, and perhaps develop some new ones, but nothing is the same without him. Arthur was a sweet gentle man, and we had a good life together. I loved him dearly and miss him terribly. We were married forty-five years, a long time to spend side by side with someone. When someone you have loved for so long goes, it

160

feels as though you will fall down because of the imbalance. It's like when you are on a teeter-totter perfectly balance and then suddenly, inexplicably the person on the other side jumps off and you crash to the ground with a hard thud that leaves you achy and alone.

We had four beautiful children together and he made me very happy. I never thought I would find someone like him. I didn't think I could be that happy twice in my life. I had a love in my life before Arthur. His name was Steven. We were high school sweethearts.

Steven was the tall dark and handsome type. We went to the same high school. I was in the graduating class of 1950 from Erasmus Hall High School in Brooklyn. Steven's father was in the military and his family moved around a great deal. We started dating in my senior year. There was something special about the year I was graduating. It was the half waypoint in the century. 1950! The country was coming alive, and I was seventeen and so much in love.

We would go for walks in the park, hold hands and when we dared, we would kiss under the bleachers. Sometimes we would take rides to Coney Island on the Brighton Beach line, and if we were really lucky, we would get stuck on top of the Ferris wheel. We would walk down by the beach with the waves slapping the shore and the gulls squawking above. It was pure, innocent, and we swore it would last forever. He was a junior when I was a senior, did I mention that? It was scandalous! No one dated a younger man! I was seventeen and he was just sixteen. I was his older woman, but he was so mature and worldly having moved so many times in his life. He had lived in Italy and Germany, and France and Texas and Arizona. He was the quiet type. He never really had time to make any lasting friendships since he moved so much. Steven was very strong and athletic but couldn't participate in team sports since he rarely stayed a full season. He was very bright and read a great deal. Books were something he could take with him no matter where he went.

161

We would stop by a shady rock near the beach and discuss life and nature and the world around us. He helped me to see that one person could make a difference in this world. He was determined, and I knew he would make a positive contribution no matter what he did. We discussed Emerson, and Thoreau and he was a big fan of Bronson Alcott. Bronson was Louisa May Alcott's father, but also the father of the modern education system. Steven dreamed of becoming a teacher. He wanted a job that was stable and secure and would keep him grounded...he had already done enough moving around for one lifetime. The excitement of the enlisted lifestyle held no fascination for him. I knew he would be a fabulous teacher since he had taught me so much.

I graduated high school and the following September started commuting by subway to NYU. I was studying to become a teacher. We thought it would be wonderful to have the same career and the same time off. We dreamed of spending our summers together just enjoying the warm weather taking long walks in the country and strolling along beautiful beaches. While I was in school, we could get together only on the weekends. We were not able to speak much during the week since I had so much schoolwork to do, but when we did see each other, it was as if time was kind enough to stop for us so we could savor every moment.

One beautiful October day we went on one of our walks. It was the kind of day where you treasure every minute because soon it would be cold and gray, and you wouldn't see sunshine again until April. We went to one of our favorite spots, on the boardwalk at Coney Island. It was deserted; unlike just two months ago when it was bustling with happy hot dog eating fathers, children clutching tickets for the Cyclone, and moms carrying some huge stuffed animal won for three times what it would have cost to buy it. We were certainly not complaining about having some time alone.

Steven was a romantic. I knew he dreamed of nothing more than having a quiet life with a stable family, not the vagabond life he had grown up with. Most boys his age dreamt of adventures and getting away from home. Steven dreamt of building a safe, warm home and letting each happy, but quiet day be an adventure. His next outburst didn't surprise me in the least. I had been reading it in his eyes for the past year; he just now was finally uttering his constant thoughts. "Mary, when I get out of school, let's get married."

Well, of course I accepted, and joy wrapped itself around me like a blanket. This fantasy kept me going. We talked about getting married and settling in a cozy little house and having children and sharing our lives together. It was an ordinary kind of life we dreamt of, but to both of us, it sounded like bliss.

We counted the days until he would graduate high school and we would be able to start our dream life. I truly wanted to live in my fantasy world, but the whole time I was with Steven I had one fear. It was so terrifying I didn't even let myself think about it. Every time it crept into my mind, I swatted it away like an unwanted fly buzzing around some impossibly delicious dessert. One day, at the beginning of Steven's senior year, that fly finally landed on my cake.

"Mary, we have to talk."

"What is it, Steven?" I knew before he said a word what was coming next. The only danger in a friendship like ours was that it might end.

"Mary, I have to go. My father is being transferred to Austria. I begged him to let me stay, but I'm just sixteen. He said I couldn't stay until I am eighteen. I hate him, I hate this. I want us to be married; I want to live with you forever. How can this be happening? Please promise me you will wait for me. I will wait for you. On my eighteenth birthday, I will

163

come back for you, I swear it, Mary."

Even though I had been trying to prepare myself for this news, it still shocked me. All I could squeeze out of my throat was "I love you, Steven,"

"I love you too, Mary." He took my hand and kissed it gently. Then he took a ring off his finger that he always wore. It belonged to his great-grandfather who fought in the Civil War. He put it on my index finger, which was the only finger it would fit on. To this day I have not taken that ring off. I never saw Steven again. He left for Austria, we exchanged cards and letters, but eventually they started dwindling. After a year I met Arthur and fell in love again. I wrote to Steven saying that I would never forget him, but I had to move on with my life. I explained about Steven to my Arthur. He understood how important a first love is, and never asked me to remove the ring, nor did he act jealous. Arthur knew that I loved him dearly and the fact that he let me keep my sweet memories of Steven made me love him even more.

I guess being in this beautiful woodland setting of Concord had me getting nostalgic and thinking of my two loves. Arthur would have loved it here. He loved to fish and was quite the outdoorsman. The pond would have been a magnet for him. I could see him drawing ever closer with his pole casting into the crisp clearness patiently waiting for his prize at the end of the string to come. I was so anxious to see the pond, that I made it my first stop as soon as I got into Concord. I didn't even go to my room at the Concord Academy first, just straight to the pond. I have never seen water quite so transparent before. There was almost an iridescent quality about it. Only the hardest, most jaded person could look out on this water and not be affected.

It was a beautiful July day with the temperature in the low eighties and a very slight breeze blowing by the water. Many were on the small beach that occupies a portion of the pond. There was absolutely no garbage or debris on the beach. Coming from Brooklyn, old tires and coffee cups and oil slicks are part of the beachscape, but there was none of that. Not a cigarette butt, not a gum wrapper. The only litter were the pinecones that fell onto the walking path around the pond.

I ventured a bit further and saw a woman going towards the water with her golden retriever in tow. I was so delighted to see this dog. It reminded me of the dog I had as a young girl. I used to walk Scout down to the beach and he would go splashing and bounding into the surf barking happily and then give me a shower as he shook the water off his coat. I watched this pair expecting to see that scene replayed here a half century later. Instead the dog went down to the water, stood with just its front paws in the very gently lapping pond, looking out into the mirror-like vastness. He looked up at his owner who was also looking out over the water. The dog again moved his head towards the pond but stood still with a reverence for this pond and the powers that created him as well as this beautiful marvel of nature. He looked up at his owner again with what I imagined to be a look of thanks for taking him to this beautiful place. The pond evoked respect not just from humans.

Thoreau wrote,

"Walden is blue at one time and green at another, even from the same point of view. Lying between the earth and the heavens it partakes of the color of both."

I had caught it on one of those half blue half green days and I got the feeling that I was standing on the shores somewhere between heaven and earth and not being completely able to distinguish between the two.

Steven would have loved this place as well. We talked about and read Thoreau and he always admired the way Thoreau was able to travel to many places without ever leaving Concord as he used to say. I have been thinking about Steven a great deal and wondering if he was even still alive.

If he was, he must be living a nice quiet life somewhere with some sweet woman who had many children for him and provided him the stability he craved.

There were so many interesting characters here in Concord. I am a rather quiet person, but I did find the people here to be friendly and I was enjoying myself immensely. There were several college professors with whom I seemed to keep meeting up with. They were very nice women about my age with whom I felt very comfortable and liked spending time with. For the most part we were on our own, but there were several group activities planned such as readings, lectures and workshops. We also ate most of our meals together.

I had retired from teaching high school English several years ago, but was still interested in learning new things, so I decided to visit the Thoreau Institute while here in Concord. All the works there are either by Thoreau or dedicated to the writings of Thoreau. I went on Friday afternoon. The Institute is a library housed in a beautiful building in the woods near the pond, and as I entered, I felt as if I was the first person on earth to visit it. Some places give you that feeling. You feel like you are a pioneer discovering a new land.

There was a rather nice-looking blind man with a cane entering a few feet ahead of me. He seemed comfortable navigating the library and I assumed he was a frequent visitor. As he walked in the young girl at the reception desk brightened up and greeted him "Hello Mr. Henry. I have the book that you asked for this morning"

"Thank you, Jennifer, don't you look lovely today!"

"Mr. Henry, you're a riot!" She said with a giggle.

I thought this was rather cute the way he was able to joke about his disability. After he sat down with his Braille book, I asked the girl at the desk about him. "That man certainly has a good attitude."

"Yes, That's David Henry, the author. He comes in almost every day to do research. He's working on another book now. We all love him. He lives right here in Concord on Sudbury Road. It's amazing how he has overcome his handicap."

"I love his work!" I've read several of his books and found a great depth of feeling and had such a connection with them. I never knew he was blind. "Do you think he would mind if I said hello?"

"Definitely not, in fact, he's a bit of a ham. He likes it when people recognize him. He's such a nice man."

"Thanks, then I will" I'm usually not one to be so bold, but I was a big fan of his writing and I would regret it if I missed this opportunity to meet one of my favorite authors. I moved towards the table he was sitting at. It was a very large square heavy oak table with a wooden mosaic in the center. It was in a room with rich wood bookshelves that contained copies of all of Thoreau's work. There were glass bookcases that contained rare editions of Thoreau's original work. Above each glass bookcase there was carved the name of the work contained in the glass case such as *Cape Cod*, *Walking*, and *Civil Disobedience*. The room had a very light and airy feeling in spite of its dark paneling, due in part to wherever there weren't bookshelves there were windows; big, beautiful wrap-around windows that when you looked out them you saw nothing but trees. You almost got the feeling you were in some very sophisticated tree house.

I tried not to speak loudly since this was a library. He hadn't yet opened his book and seemed to be searching through his backpack setting up some sort of a contraption that looked like a small computer with no

167

screen. Before I had the chance to launch into what would surely sound like the ramblings of a gushing bobbysoxer–type fan he spoke.

"Excuse me, but can you tell me if there is an electrical outlet nearby? I usually keep this thing charged, but it seems to have lost power and I will have to plug it in."

"Yes, there's an outlet right behind you. I can plug that in for you."

"Thank you, Miss, that would be very kind of you."

I could feel myself blush a bit as he called me Miss. It had been quite some time since I was called Miss. As I moved in closer to him, I noticed that he looked a bit startled. I apologized, and said I hoped I hadn't caught him off guard. How insensitive of me to not move very gingerly near a blind person. "No, that's not it, it's just your perfume…Arpege isn't it? I haven't smelt that in almost 50 years."

"Well, you do have an amazing sense of smell! That is exactly what I am wearing. I have been wearing it since I was a teenager!" I decided to fess up that I knew his identity. "I am a big fan of yours, Mr. Henry. Your books are among my favorites. In fact, I used to teach "_Where the Path Ends_" in one of my high school literature classes."

"So, you know who I am?"

"Yes, the girl at the front desk told me you were David Henry. I feel like a silly schoolgirl."

"You were never a silly schoolgirl…I mean I am sure you were never a silly schoolgirl"

"Do you mind if I sit down?" I asked.

168

"No, please do. I am at a disadvantage…what is your name?"

"Oh, forgive me, my name is Mary Sewall." I extended my hand to find his so he would know I wanted to shake it. As our hands touched, I looked at his face, and something strange came over me. It was a familiarity. It was a feeling that I knew him…in fact I was sure of it! This was my Steven. I would swear it! But how could it be he called himself David Henry? He obviously didn't know it was me since he couldn't see me. What if I was wrong? What if it wasn't him? I would feel like such a fool. Besides, I didn't want to risk insulting him if he were not Steven. I decided to just wait and see if he realized it was me. If he didn't, then I would take it as a sign that either he wasn't my Steven, or he was, and just didn't know me anymore. Either would be hard to deal with, but I would prefer the former to the later. He squeezed my hand slightly and I felt him linger for a moment on my ring. Perhaps wishful thinking, but I thought I saw a look of recognition cross his face. I was letting my imagination run away with me. If this really was my Steven, he would have no doubt in his mind, blind or not that it was me. But then, I should have no doubt as to his identity either, and I did. This was all getting to be too strange for me. I had to get some fresh air. "I've taken up enough of your time Mr. Henry. I should let you get back to your work."

"Oh, you haven't disturbed me a bit Ms. Sewall. Perhaps if you have some time, we could discuss how you have taught my book. I would love to hear what you think about it."

"I would like that very much; it was very nice meeting you."

"Likewise, Ms. Sewall."

As I walked away, I could feel him looking in my direction, his eyes, though only seeing darkness followed me out the library as if they could actually see me clearly. I now had no doubt in my mind that this was Steven. There was just no point in telling him who I was since he didn't recognize me.

I thought about him for the rest of the day. Here he was, the man I had loved fifty years ago right here next to me, and yet it was as if he still was a missing person to me. He recognized my perfume, but thousands of women wear Arpege, so it wasn't exactly as though I had a patent on that scent. He could have remembered he once loved a girl named Mary, but again, that is such a common name among women my age, and he never knew Arthur or that his last name was Sewall. He could have recognized the ring, but that was probably my imagination. He was a famous writer, and I was sure he forgot about me right after my last letter. He had so much going for him, why would he have ever spent a second thinking about me?

It made perfect sense that he chose this pseudonym. David Henry was Henry David backwards and I am sure he did it in tribute to Thoreau. That would be so like Steven. His books were full of adventure and exciting locals many of which I now remember him telling me he lived in as a child. I wondered if he had gone back to these places, or relied on his memories and wrote from the peaceful, quiet setting he always dreamed of? I wondered if he had married. Was he still married? This was another reason why I could not approach him. There was also a piece of me that felt guilty for the way I told him good-bye. I regretted having sent him a "Dear John" letter and would have liked to have told him in person, I felt I owed him at least that much. I wondered all these years if he hated me. If he ever saw me again would he spit in my face and tell me how much he hated me for not waiting for him? Would he be angry? How did he deal with it? Ironically, now thinking about the writings of David Henry, there was always a female character that was not drawn very flatteringly. She remained unattainable and cold. Was this me? Was this how he saw me, and how he felt about what I did to him? Did he choose to eviscerate me for all eternity through his writings? Through writing, he could create a character that he could manipulate into doing exactly what he wanted instead of the way life really turned out where I did exactly what he didn't want me to do.

Again, my head was spinning. I decided to go for a short walk before heading back to the Concord Academy to lie down before dinner. When I arrived at my room, less than an hour from meeting Steven, there was a package lying beside my door. I opened it to find a copy of _"Where the Path Ends"_ with the inscription "To Mary, thanks for being one of my biggest fans...Always, David Henry."

I just stared at it as if it would start talking to me. I looked around, but there was no one around. He couldn't have gotten here this quickly, and with his blindness it is doubtful he did this himself, but the librarian did tell me he lived here in Concord, and probably had many people who could help him pull off such a miracle. I was extremely impressed and decided that even if he didn't recognize me, I had to spend time with him, if nothing else, because he was a famous author whom I admired and I would love to speak with him about his writing having taught it for so many years.

I called the library, asked for the front desk receptionist to see if she knew how I could get in touch with Mr. Henry to thank him for a gift. She said he was expecting my call and asked me to hold on for one minute. Before I realized what was happening I heard the tapping of her shoes on the hardwood floors as she brought the cordless phone over to him...at least that is how I envisioned it in my mind, because before I lost my nerve and hung up I heard... "Hello Ms. Sewall."

"Hello, Mr. Henry." I sputtered, "Thank you so much for the book."

"You are quite welcome. I don't often get to meet someone who has been teaching my work to others, and I would love to find out how you interpreted some of my more elusive passages. Would you mind having dinner with me this evening and perhaps we can discuss it further?"

I felt fifty years slip away from my body and right off the calendar. I was back in Brooklyn in 1950 with the waves slapping the shore, the gulls squawking above me, and holding Steven's hand. Wings fluttered in my stomach as he spoke. The butterflies that had been cocooning in there for the last fifty years decided to finally break free. I had signed up for the group dinner this evening, but I was not going to let this chance to spend time with Steven pass me by again, even if he didn't know it was me. "Yes, I would like that."

"Good, can I have my driver pick you up at the Academy at six?"

"How did you know, by the way, that I was staying at the Academy?" I asked, hoping he would divulge his spy technique.

"Oh, we in Concord are very used to the onslaught of new visitors every year the second weekend in July, and most stay at the Academy, so it was really not too hard to figure out."

"Well, you are quite resourceful. I will look forward to dinner."

"Yes, likewise."

As I hung up the phone, I nearly collapsed on the bed with a sudden dizzy feeling whirring around in my head. It felt like a few years ago when I had a bout of vertigo, only this was a nice feeling. I am sixty-eight years old. How can I possibly be behaving like a teenager? How did he do this to me? Steven? David Henry? Whoever he was, or wanted to be, I was going to enjoy this evening and live life again.

Ok. It's 4:30. I have time for a quick shower and change before the driver comes to get me. I hadn't really brought anything fancy to wear, so I hoped that whatever I had would be good enough. I had a skirt and a nice cotton top I was going to wear tonight for the dinner anyway, so that would have to do. I showered and dotted on my Arpege the same way I have for the past fifty years, a drop behind each ear and a drop behind each knee. As I slipped on the skirt, I noticed the size tag. It was a 12. Back when I knew Steven, I was a size 4! My, so much time has gone by. Would he still find me attractive? What am I saying, he can't see me! It would make no difference what I looked like or what size I was.

David Chapter 28

"The only danger in Friendship is that it will end." Henry David Thoreau.

There was no doubt in my mind it was her. When she extended her hand to me and I touched the ring it was the clincher. I felt the signet from my great grandfather's ring and knew this was my Mary. This was the woman I had longed to be with for the last fifty years. This was the woman I had dreamt about, wrote about, and prayed about for the last fifty years. I was so stunned and off balance the moment I smelled her Arpege. There was no one who could wear Arpege the way Mary did. She used to dot it behind her ears and her knees. Don't ask me why, that's just how she did it. It would drive me wild when I was seventeen, and now at sixty-seven it was having the same effect on me. Here she was, back in my life again, but with a hitch…she does not recognize me. Or worse yet, she recognizes me, but does not want to confess she does, because she does not find me attractive anymore, or does not want to be saddled with a blind man. Could I be wrong? Could it just be another Mary who wears Arpege? No. I have felt her presence for the last half century. She was back in my life and even without sight, my other senses were well aware of her. The scent was undoubtedly Mary. Her voice, though now a bit creakier and mature was the same. It could still melt me. The contours of her hand, I had memorized its shape and even though the skin was a bit softer and velvety rather than firm and smooth as it was fifty years ago, I still knew the contours of her hand and this was Mary's hand.

I haven't been able to marry another, because no one could compare to her. I couldn't blame her for moving on. She was so loving and vivacious it was a given that someone else would sweep her off her feet before I got back. I knew as I said good-bye to her that there was no way she would still be there when I got back. It was like leaving a diamond necklace in a room full of thieves and expecting it to be there when you returned. It was my own fault for leaving her behind and I never blamed her. By some miracle, here she was back in my life and I could not let this second chance to spend some time with her go by. I just wish she knew it was me. How wonderful it would be if we could just turn back the clock to fifty years ago and melt into each other's arms the way we did back then. How wonderful it would be if she would say 'Steven, I know it's you, I love you and blind or not, I want you to marry me, just like you promised all those years ago'. That's the danger of being a writer. You are always writing happy endings to stories that can't possibly have one.

Maybe it just wasn't meant to be with me and Mary. Maybe God had a reason for separating us all those years ago and I shouldn't question His plan. Maybe she would have broken my heart, or me hers, and we would have hated each other. Maybe some sort of tragedy would have befallen us if we had married, like one of us would have been seriously ill, or we would have lost a child, or had any number of horrible things happen to us. The only thing that has gotten me through these past fifty years was the belief that God knows what He is doing. I still indulged in a healthy dose of 'what might have been', but I was able to accept our fate because I believed it happened for a reason. Just like I believed her coming here to Concord was for a reason. I feel we were destined to meet again and maybe this time we are ready for each other. Maybe I could not have become a writer without having experienced the angst of losing Mary.

Somewhere in the recesses of my brain I always thought I would see Mary again, and in fact my biggest fear was that I would die without having seen her again. I am not afraid of dying, I feel each day is a learning experience and unlike my inverted pseudo-namesake I believe you will never be smarter than you are on the day you die. My fear was that I would live and not see her again. In a way, that fear became a reality the day I lost my sight, but she is here before me now and even if I cannot physically see her, I see her. Her being here in Concord puts flesh and bones around the soul I have shared a piece of for the past fifty years.

I do not think losing my sight hurt as much as losing Mary did. I had sight for over fifty years, I have a great memory and can engage it to draw me a picture of whatever I need to see in my mind's eye. But I only had Mary for a year. That was not enough time to spend with one who you love the way I loved Mary. I tried to picture us together in different places seeing different things. Sometimes I could, sometimes I could not. When I could not, I would get frustrated and upset and try to banish all thoughts of Mary from my mind, but that was too painful, so instead I invited her memory to take up permanent residence in my soul. I had married Mary a long time ago in my heart. To marry anyone else would have made me a bigamist.

I am certainly not the same man I was all those years ago, and perhaps it is best she gets to know David Henry and that she keeps Steven as just a memory. I decided to just let fate rule this evening and that I would be David Henry, and if she realized I was Steven and wanted to acknowledge that fact, great. If she realized I was Steven, but couldn't handle it, and pretended not to know, I would accept that too as her decision. If she really didn't realize I was Steven, and I was just a blip on the radar screen of her life and didn't mean as much to her as she had to me, I would have to accept that as well.

I took very special care preparing for this evening. I had not been out with a woman since the ninth decade of last century, so I was a bit out of practice. I assumed the nineties hadn't changed things too severely, so I went by the golden rule of dating…be clean, be nice and be on time. I had a gentleman who lived with me and helped me around the house and drove me places. Ralph was his name. He had been my companion ever since I lost my sight. He was as giddy as I was at the prospect of me having a date. I didn't tell him it was Mary. I had babbled on and on incessantly about Mary in the past, but until I knew how she felt in the here and now, in the year 2000, I was not going to get my hopes up or Ralph's hopes up either. He lived vicariously through my stories of Mary.

176

I didn't want him to be vicariously heartbroken if that was to be my fate.

This must have been the week for me to relive my past. I had an old student of mine drop by this week. It was back when I was teaching at Texas Tech and I had this rough and tumble football player named Chris Steele in my Sophomore creative writing class. He started off so bad but got so good. I like to think of him as being one of my greatest successes as a teacher. He went on to become a famous singer-songwriter in Nashville and is wildly successful. He came to visit me in the hopes of getting back to his creative roots. When he started writing it was with much loftier thoughts and somehow sold out and was writing what he felt was inferior, mass appealing rather than self-appealing work.

My advice to Chris was that he needed to remain true to himself and maybe I should take my own advice tonight with Mary. I should be honest with her about who I am. If she likes me the way I am, great, if she does not, at least I will be able to live with myself and know I was honest.

It was getting closer to six pm and Ralph was ready to pick up Mary. I thought I would take her to the Colonial Inn, the nicest restaurant in Concord. There was a little common area at the Academy where Mary was waiting for Ralph and me. It was kind of her to not make me have to navigate the staircase. That was so like Mary. I knew she was there the second I walked through the door; I could smell her Arpege.

"Hello, Mary."

"Hello Mr. Henry."

"Please call me David."

"OK…David."

I should have said 'Please call me Steven,' but I wasn't ready yet.

"I thought we'd go to the Colonial Inn. It's right in Concord and it's one of my favorites. It's said that Emerson and Thoreau used to eat there all the time."

"Really?"

"Well, that's what they say, but it could just be a little Concord folklore. I am dying to hear your interpretation of _"Where the Path Ends."_ It was probably my favorite book even though it was not a fan favorite. It received a good deal of critical acclaim but wasn't a best seller."

"I really thought it was one of your best works. I found I could relate to it on many different levels. Your main character, a boy who has no roots and spends his life regretting a love he left behind, I once knew a boy like that." She answered.

"Did you? What became of him?"

"I don't know. He was my first love, and we parted never to see each other again. There is not a day that goes by though when I don't wonder what became of him."

My heart skipped a beat. She thought of me every day! I could not believe what I was hearing. This was what I had lived for this past half century. This was the moment I thought would never happen in real life, so I had to create it over and over again in my books. Now here it was, and I can see I did not do it justice. No words I have ever written could describe the sheer joy in my heart at this moment knowing she had not forgotten about me.

I would have to compose myself. I never cursed my blindness. I always look at every attribute we have as a gift from God and I thought my blindness made me appreciate beauty in other ways that sighted people might overlook. But right now, I wanted so badly to be able to read the look in her eyes. This was so uneven. I was seeing in my mind Mary at age eighteen. She was seeing me at sixty-seven. She could see the here and now, I could only see the past. I tried to pull myself back into the here and now and asked her, "So what did you think of the female lead in the book?"

"I actually thought she was a very unsympathetic figure. She seemed to hurt the male character very deeply and be the source of most of his angst. She didn't seem to have much of a heart."

"Oh, no, that wasn't my intent at all!" I was crushed. I did not want her to think I was taking revenge out on her through the book. In fact, I thought I had drawn that character to be strong, and a survivor, not cold and heartless. I told her this and added, "I thought she was coping best she could given the circumstances. It was all the boy's fault for leaving her. She did not push him away in any manner. It was entirely his fault."

"My take on it was that she hurt him deeply and he would have been better off if he never knew her."

"But then they wouldn't have had the wonderful time together that they did have. Isn't it better to have had that kind of love in your life once even if it goes away than to never have experienced that kind of love?" I asked her of course hoping that the answer from her would be yes. I did not want to think that Mary thought our time together was a mistake or a tragedy. It was a blessing that we had each other to love even if it was brief.

"I do feel that everything happens for a reason and we shouldn't question it." She answered.

I thought I might pry a little further into her mind trying to figure out if she knew it was me. "Do you think you came here for a reason?"

"Absolutely. I knew the moment I first gazed over Walden Pond that this was a magical place and something wonderful would happen to me here."

That was such a typical honest, Mary answer. Most people cannot express their feelings as openly as she can. I could not stand the suspense any longer. Our waitress had just placed the entrees before us, and I knew I could not eat a bite if I did not ask this last question. "Do you think something wonderful has happened to you here?"

The scent of Arpege enveloped me, as a feeling of peace and warmth shot through me when she touched my hand and said, "Yes, Steven, it has."

Ted Chapter 29

This had been a tense year at work with all the Y2K nonsense. It was a tough time to be a computer programmer. Everyone was predicting the world would come to a screeching halt as the clock struck midnight and the new century dawned. I needed a break. I hadn't been on a vacation since I was with Sharon, and now the separation was going on almost seven years. I had taken a few little camping trips with the girls, but I felt I needed to do something by myself, to just get away alone and think. I had always been a big fan of Thoreau and someone at work told me about a Thoreau weekend in Concord, Mass that they went to once that was both peaceful and intellectually stimulating. I decided this was something I should do. It was the second weekend in July, which coincided with the girls being at camp so it would work out perfectly.

The drive up to Massachusetts from South Salem was really nice. It took about three and a half hours. The group that sponsored this weekend was the Thoreau Society. I joined it and I participated in some of the group activities. There were lectures, and readings and walks through Walden Woods. It was very inspirational being there. I felt at peace and a calmness come over me as soon as I arrived in Concord. There was something very otherworldly about this place. It brought back memories of the back forty and the peace and calm I had on the farm and of my childhood when things were simpler, and life was non-demanding. I longed to go back to those days. I hated what my life had become. I truly felt I was spinning out of control. Sharon was holding me hostage with her demands. I just wanted to be free again, but I couldn't seem to escape her grip. I was lonely, but I didn't want to let anyone in. I built a wall around myself and was hesitant to start tearing any of the bricks down. Instead I kept building the wall higher and higher. Here I felt safe. I felt as though I could start to tear down the wall a bit and join the humans again.

One of the events was a dinner that was followed by the keynote speech on Saturday night. I got there a little late, I never get anywhere on time because it takes me so long to decide what to wear and I always have to check a few times to make sure I shut everything off, and didn't forget to bring something with me that would no doubt prove to be something indispensable later in the evening once I noticed its absence. It was a pretty packed house. The dinner was held in the basement of The First Parish Church. It was a bit of a claustrophobic room with low ceilings and high windows. The only free seat I could spot was at a table with a bunch of ladies. Most were older, schoolteacher types. I had met a lot of teachers on my trip here. I asked the woman I would be sitting next to if the seat was taken, she said it wasn't, and when she turned around, I noticed how pretty she was. She had cocoa-brown hair and beautiful big brown soulful eyes. I figured this was going to be a good dinner.

"Hi, I'm Ted," I said as a general greeting to the table. The woman who was sitting at the helm made the introductions going all around the table, and I paid no real attention until she got to the girl I was sitting next to.

"…And that's Lucy."

"Hi Lucy, gee I hope I'm not going to be tested, I will never remember anybody's name!" All the ladies giggled, and I started on my clam chowder. It was a bit salty, but not altogether bad. All the ladies at the table were rather chatty, but Lucy was sort of quiet. I decided I would attempt some small talk. "So where are you from?"

"Originally, I was from New Jersey, but moved to Eastchester, NY about 12 years ago."

She had this great voice. It was very soft and sexy, with just a hint of Jersey. It was just like her. If you closed your eyes and just heard her

182

speak you would be able to picture her exactly. I didn't want to close my eyes, though, because the view was just too nice. "No kidding, I live in Westchester too! I was originally from upstate NY, but now live in South Salem."

"Well, that's a coincidence! Are you a teacher? She asked.

"No, I guess I would fall into the category of being just a Thoreau fan. I never did anything like this before. I thought it would be a nice restful retreat. Are you a teacher?" I asked.

"No, just a fan as well. I'm hoping to come away from this with some inspiration to do some writing. I have always dabbled in writing, and thought it would be my career one day, but life just sort of happened and I never got around to it." As she talked, I just couldn't take my eyes off her.

"So, what do you do?" I asked.

"I have my own business, a chocolate shop."

"Oh, wow, that sounds fattening! How do you stay in such great shape?" I hoped after I said it she wouldn't get scared off by my blatant flirting.

"Well, when you are around it all the time, even the most tempting things get uninteresting." She said.

"I know exactly what you mean…" I had Sharon on my mind.

"So, what do you do, Ted?" I loved the way she said my name. It's such a dull name. Ted, it rhymes with dead. But she seemed to breathe life in it and made it sound virile and exiting. I almost forgot the question…oh yes…what do I do?

"I am a computer programmer."

"Wow, I have no head for computers at all. I still keep my books in a ledger. My accountant goes wild! I did just treat myself to a laptop. I hope it will give me the push I need to write something."

We chatted effortlessly through dinner. Occasionally we remembered it wasn't a table for two and included someone else in our conversation or joined another conversation going on at a different corner of the table. But I kept getting drawn back to her. There was something about her. Something I hadn't felt in over a decade. Something I don't think I ever felt with Sharon. It was beyond lust. It was a connection. It was those soulful big brown eyes. They seemed vaguely familiar. I could just get lost in them.

"Are you going to the keynote address?" She asked.

"Yes, I was planning to, are you?"

"Yes," she replied.

"Come on, I'll walk over with you" I sat next to her in the church's meeting room where the speaker would deliver his speech. When we got there, she saw a girl that she identified as her roommate and went over to her. "Hi, Faith, this is Ted, he lives not too far from me in NY."

"Hi Ted, nice to meet you, would you like to sit with us?" I thought she was going to be the third wheel, but quickly realized I was. I had come to the party late, and Lucy had already made her friends up here. If I wanted to be close to her, I would have to follow her lead.

"Sure, that's very nice of you." I mustered all my graciousness to squeeze that one out. As if she owned the room! I didn't like this chick. She made me feel extremely uncomfortable. We sat three in the pew and at least I was able to finagle the seating so I was next to Lucy and not Faith. She smelled so good. I have no idea what the scent was. It was some really nice perfume, and you could tell it was expensive. It wasn't the cheap stuff Sharon wears. In fact, nothing about her was cheap or trashy. She was so different from Sharon. She was all class; Sharon was all brass.

The address was on Thoreau's influence as the father of modern-day environmentalism. I would have probably found it fascinating if I was able to concentrate on it, but my thoughts were only on one thing. What was she wearing under those Capri pants and that sweater set? There I go again, fantasizing on what lies beneath…. Okay, cool it…I better pay attention. This woman was really smart and would lose interest in me if I couldn't hold an intelligent conversation after this speech so I needed to focus…environmentalism…blah blah blah…conflict between nature and civilization…yada, yada, yada…preserving the health of our biosphere…yeah, okay, whatever…. Is it over yet? Can I walk her home? Will the roommate be hanging around? So many questions.

I was pulled back to reality by the sound of the applause rising up through the hall.

"Wasn't that great? She asked.

"Yes, I've always thought that Thoreau held the key for reconciling the conflict between nature and civilization." Whoa! Where did I pull that one from? Sometimes I even amaze myself. She was quite impressed, I could tell.

"Yes, that is exactly how I feel. It's rare to meet anyone passionate about the environment. I'm really glad I met you, Ted." Oh man, she said my name again! I just wanted to scoop her up and drag her back to my hotel room and not come out until Monday! I can't believe I am having these feelings! I have not been with a woman since the night Sharon and I conceived Nancy and that's going on 12 years ago! I had totally shut that part of my life down but here it was, springing back to life again…literally! I better get under control, or I would totally embarrass myself. I didn't want to scare her off. "Well, I'm really beat." She said. "I did a lot of walking today and I think I am going to turn in. Faith and I are staying at the Concord Academy, are you there too?"

"No, I took a hotel room a few miles south of here. I should have done the whole gathering thing, but I booked kind of late." Damn! I could have been staying in the same place she was if I hadn't taken so long to make a commitment to come here. It would have been just like college. I could have snuck down the hall and caught a glimpse of her sleeping, or brushing her teeth, or doing her morning exercises…. oh stop! I have to stop this, or I'll never get through the weekend.

"Ok, well, we'll probably see you in the morning, if you are going to the group breakfast."

"Yes, I'm looking forward to it." Damn, I better find out if I can register for that. I hope it's not too late… "See you in the morning. Good night, Faith" I thought I heard a grumble. I could tell Faith liked me as much as I liked her. From the very first time I saw her, I knew she hated me. It didn't matter; Lucy was the only one I cared about at this moment. I watched the two of them walk towards the Academy. I was a bit scared of my feelings, but also exuberant and delighted that I still was capable of having these feelings. And she's right in Westchester! How good is that? Before we leave, I will get her number and ask her out for next weekend.

Everyone gathered the next morning for breakfast in the hall of this little church. I got there extra early so I could pay twice as much money and make sure they would let me in, and I could save a seat for Lucy and magnanimously, Faith. I was waiting almost a half hour and had to endure some philosophy professor who caught my ear drone on about transcendentalism and how the only limitation in finding God is not finding yourself. Oh please, I was raised a very strict Catholic. I went to Catholic School. I had found God a long time ago. In fact, we had such a good relationship, I didn't bother Him, and He didn't bother me. If you ask me now what religion I am I would have to say I am a practicing 'good person'. I try to not break any laws and keep to myself. God knows I've been keeping chaste and celibate, but with a little luck, that would all start to change soon.

Before this guy totally put me to sleep, she came in. Her sidekick was right in tow, but all I could see was Lucy. She looked fantastic. It was a really hot morning, the kind of morning you get when you know you are just going to die by noon. She looked like this precious, cool, flower. She had on this long sundress, and her dark hair pulled back in a ponytail. She looked so much younger than her age. If she hadn't mentioned having two teenagers last night, I would have thought she was barely in her twenties. Her skin was creamy white, like the unpasteurized milk straight from the cow I was forbidden to drink. Her gorgeous eyes just lit up the room. She was so totally awesome. She stopped to talk to a few people on her way into the room. She had already made so many friends up here. Everybody knew her name, and everybody seemed to love her. There was just something about her.

I heard her say to a few people to be sure they give her their address so she could send them some chocolate when she got back home. I suppose for even a normal woman the promise of chocolate would contribute to their popularity, but honestly, she didn't even need to offer anything but her own sweet self to make people like her.

Finally, I caught her eye, and she gave me a shy wave and tried to split through the crowd towards me. I could see Faith's look of annoyance. If

187

she had any say, I knew I had a snowball's chance in hell of getting Lucy to sit by me. I started to move towards them. "Hi Ladies, how are you this morning? You both look so cool and refreshed on such a hot morning" Honestly, I couldn't tell you what Faith was wearing and whether she was cool and refreshed or not, I just didn't want to be so blatant as to only compliment my Lucy. I think Faith was wearing clothes or something... "I saved you both a seat. Why don't you put your purses down, and go up to the buffet, I'll watch them for you?"

"Oh, thanks!" Said my Lucy.

"I'll take mine with me." Said the bitch. They made their way to the buffet line and started to fill their plates. It seemed to take them forever to get back. I just couldn't take my eyes off her. Finally, they returned and fortunately, Lucy slipped into the seat next to me. Unfortunately, that meant I had to sit across from Faith at the table for four and endure her eyes throwing daggers at me. I was able to sit next to my Lucy though, and smell her wonderful perfume. The God that guy had been talking about earlier must have been on my side, because this old guy comes up to the table and asked if the empty seat was taken and if he could join us. I said "sure!" This was great! He could occupy what's-her-name while I focused on the object of my desires.

"So, Lucy, tell me about your kids? A boy and a girl you said?" She brightened up and started to go on and on about Varsity baseball and yearbook and whatever, whatever. I was just studying the way her mouth moved around each word and how delicious her lips looked. She asked me if I was going to eat. I told her I had gotten here early and already had eaten, but to not let me stop her. She started to take bites of her now cold scrambled eggs, and little nibbles of a blueberry muffin. "So, what are your plans for today? Are you and Faith going to the reading at noon?" Please say no, please say no, please say no....

" I'm going, but Faith is going on the tour of Emerson's home."
YESSSSSSSSS!!!!! I hoped the sheer glee in my heart wasn't shining through.

"Before the reading I was going to maybe walk around the town a bit and see if I could pick up some souvenirs for my girls. Would you like to join me?" I asked. Faith shot me an evil look and I shot her one right back. I wasn't sure why this chick hated me so much, but it didn't matter, as long as Lucy liked me. She seemed to hesitate for a few moments, but said she would go shopping with me, so I guess she did like me. We mulled around in the church hall a bit after the breakfast and I couldn't wait to get her alone and out into the open. The room was the same one dinner had been in the night before, in a basement of a church about 200 years old and was really claustrophobically confining. If it weren't that I knew I would see her there, I probably would have turned around and left the room as soon as I got there.

I felt so good once I was out with her in the fresh air. All I could feel was her presence next to me. All I could smell was her perfume. All I could taste were her lips that I was imagining touching mine. All I could hear was her soft, sexy voice whispering my name. I started telling her all about my girls, and about my work and my childhood on the farm and my nine brothers and sisters, and my pet birds, and my ex-wife, well, almost ex-wife, and my love of camping and my several broken bones mostly due to accidents. I must have gone on and on forever not coming up for air, but it had been so long since I had spoken with an adult human being. She patiently listened to everything I said and commented at just the right times and laughed at just the right times. She was wonderful. Someone I could really talk to and open up to. I guess the eight years I had been alone I had been saving up for someone special to share things with, and she was the one. We were walking very slowly towards town. We had about two hours to kill so I wanted to savor every moment.

She asked me if I wanted to go to mass Sunday morning with her and Faith. I told her I used to go but I don't go anymore because I saw all the hypocrites at mass that I knew were sinners and yet were there at mass. She had a different way of looking at it because she said, "Isn't that the point? I always thought the message of the Catholic Church was that no matter what you had done in the past as long as you asked for forgiveness, you were forgiven and welcomed back with open arms. At least that's how I interpret it. So maybe those who you call sinners have a very good reason for being there."

"You have a very interesting way of looking at things, Lucy. I just feel uncomfortable there lately. I don't know why."

"That's okay, I just thought I'd ask if you'd like to join me. I'll be driving back right after mass because I have to pick up my kids at my Mom's house in New Jersey, so I guess I won't see you after tonight."

"I was hoping we could see each other when we got back home. Can I call you? Maybe we can go out to dinner next weekend?"

"Sure, that would be nice. I'd like that." She had the nicest smile on her face when she said this.

Lucy Chapter 30

I have this love/hate relationship with my new cell phone. I am happy to be able to keep in touch with my kids and be just a phone call away if they should ever need me, but it also can be jarring when it rings and you are not expecting a call. Mom is a very hands-off person, so I was not expecting a call or update on the kids while she watched them. When it rang and I saw mom's number I had an immediate sense of dread that something was wrong. "Hi, Mom, what's up"

I heard my daughter's sweet voice on the other end. "Mom, it's Olivia, are you on your way home?"
"Yes, sweetheart I am at a rest stop on the turnpike, I should be home within the hour. Is everything ok?"

"It is now, but there was a little problem here this weekend. Grandma and Grandpa are both fine, but in the hospital. I will fill you in when you get back. Please don't freak out, I just wanted to hear your voice."

"Olivia, are you and Joey ok? You can't leave that dangling in the air." In spite of her request, I was now panicking.

"Mom, I only called you because I didn't want you to hear it on the radio on the way home."

"On the radio??? What on earth happened??"

"Mom let me just tell you again that everybody is fine. There was a gas leak at the house, and Joey and I got grandma and grandpa out and it's all good. It's all over the news so I wanted to make sure you didn't hear it while driving. I also didn't want you to drive up and see the house. It's blocked off. We are at the hospital. You should come straight here."

My mind was racing with thoughts of my parents and children in danger. Olivia was right, if I heard this on the radio, I would have driven off the road. Much better I was prepared. I stopped at the nearest rest stop and got myself a coffee, in a poor attempt to calm down, and maybe pushed the speed limit a bit, but got back to the Shore safely. I drove straight to the hospital and Olivia met me in the lobby. I gave her a huge hug and she still had a lingering smell of gas on her clothing.

"Mom, Grandma and Grandpa are being checked out and Joey is too. He got a nasty scrape on his arm when he was dragging grandpa out of the house, but the doctor said they will all be fine. Did you see the house yet?"

"No, I came straight here.

"There is some damage, but not a total loss. I smelled something and called 911 immediately. Grandma and Grandpa were asleep, so I got Grandma, but Grandpa was unconscious, so Joey threw him over his shoulder and got him out. He was awesome. I was so proud of him."

I was still trying to process what my daughter was saying. "I'm so proud of both of you!"

"The firemen said we all would have been dead in about 5 more minutes. It was a miracle we all made it out alive. There was a small explosion and fire, but they were able to put it out right away."

I just held my beautiful baby girl and couldn't let her go. She had just saved my parents lives as well as her brother's and her own. She definitely got that heroism from her Uncle Rico. My son threw his grandfather over his shoulder? What? Another hero! I don't think I could have been any more proud of my kids.

"Let's go see your Grandparents and Joey."

I let Olivia lead me to the ER where they were all in one big room separated by curtains. My mom saw me and motioned for me to come over. She looked very pail but was strong as she squeezed my hand.

"Lucy, I'm so sorry..." I was a bit confused by her words but let her continue.

"For all these years I have treated you like you were a screw up because you got married so young and had kids so fast. I never took the time to see what an amazing job you did with these kids. They are smart, strong, selfless young people who just saved not only me and your father, but maybe the whole neighborhood from a gas explosion. I owe you an apology for all these years of resenting you and making you feel like you were a disappointment. It's you who should be disappointed in me. You are a marvelous mother, and I am not. Please forgive me."

And there they were. The words I needed to hear, but never thought I would. I felt guilty for feeling such joy.

"It's ok, Mom, I'm glad you and dad and the kids are fine. I'm also glad you got to see firsthand what I knew from the moment I first felt Olivia move inside me. I knew she was meant to be here for a very special reason."

I saw the look on my mother's face turn to shame as she remembered how harshly she treated me when I told her I was pregnant. I'm not a person who likes to see anyone sad, but it did give me a bit of satisfaction knowing I finally was validated.

"I'm going to check in on Dad and Joey."

I found my dad sleeping, but the nurse said he was stable and would make a full recovery. Sitting up in bed eating ice cream was my boy. He had his arm bandaged and was having a bit of difficulty holding the cup, so I started feeding him like I did 16 years ago when he was a baby. I kissed his forehead and sat on the edge of his bed.

"All those early morning football practices came in handy!" I said with a wink.

He squeezed my hand and said "Mom, I was so scared. Grandpa just wasn't moving, but I had to get him out, so I just threw him over my shoulder. I think it was adrenaline kicking in." Then he gave me a smile and said, "But stop sending him so much chocolate, he weighs a ton!" We both broke out in a big smile as I finished feeding him his ice cream. Sometimes even bad days can be good days.

Billy Chapter 31

I've thought about dating some women I've met now that I am single, but I still miss Lucy. They may be younger than her, but none are as beautiful, graceful, kindhearted as my Lucy. Most importantly, none of them come fully accessorized with my own children like Lucy does. I am taking my medication and I haven't lost my temper in over 9 months. That's a great accomplishment for me. I also haven't really been around other people or in a position where my hot buttons have been pushed, so I'm not sure it really is that much of an accomplishment.

Lucy used to beg me to get help. She knew my mood swings were not normal. If I had only listened to her, and not been so stubborn I could have gotten on medication sooner and maybe saved my marriage, my family and my life. Now I am just a calm, single man.

Rico's warnings to stay away from Lucy still resound in my ears all these years later. I am doing so well now; I don't want to act too quickly and blow it. I want to make a new lifelong commitment to Lucy and this time, not screw it up. The kids have been slowly coming around. They see the changes in me and hopefully are reporting favorably back to Lucy. I am trying to think of a way to show her how much I've changed and how much I love her.

I took a trip up to Boston to see my brother and thought I might stop by the pond that Lucy loved so much to see if maybe I could relive a bit of those happy Honeymoon days before my disease started to consume me. I remember during my worst episode when I hit Lucy, she wrote me a note with a Thoreau quote meant to encourage me. Instead, I got enraged by it. I crumpled it up without really reading it. I stopped by the shop near the pond to see if maybe I could get some help identifying the quote.

"Hi, can I help you?" asked the friendly back-to-nature looking girl behind the counter.

"I'm looking for a quote by Thoreau about failure but not sure about the rest of it."

She pulled her brows together, so I figured this was not going to get me anywhere. The guy wrote so much it was like looking for a needle in a haystack. Then a slight smile came across her face. "I know the one you mean. It's one of his most famous quotes and most misunderstood. We have it on a key chain."

Shop girl disappeared into the back for a half minute and came out with a small laminated key chain fob. The quote was,

"In the long run, men hit only what they aim at. Therefore, thou they should fail immediately, they'd better aim high."

"Yes! That's it!" I paid her, thanked her and walked over to the pond. I found a nice quiet spot to sit on a rock and just look out over the water the peace and calm. I was beginning to see why this place was so special to Lucy and to so many others.

I pulled out the key chain and read the words over and over until I finally got it. All I saw when Lucy first showed it to me were the words "hit" and "fail" I thought she was trying to call me a failure because of my hot temper. Had I taken the time to read it, I would have seen she was trying to be supportive as always, and encouraging me to keep going no matter what the outcome of the bar exam. She was right too. I failed the New York bar two times before passing on the third try. Now I have a good job with a firm in Manhattan. I put the keychain carefully in my pocket and pull it every day to remind me of Lucy's faith in me, and that I need to have more faith in myself.

Lucy Chapter 32

I tried to get going with my book. Being a writer himself, Chris encouraged me, but he was so busy I couldn't get the kind of motivation from him I needed. I allowed myself an occasional fantasy about what life would be like if Chris ever left the road and settled down with me, but it only made me sad to think that my soulmate belonged to the world, and not to me.

My trip to Concord had changed my life in so many ways. I had a sense of what my purpose in life was and I finally mended my fences with my parents. I met a nice guy who could have some potential. This was a good trip.

I made plans to see Ted on my first Friday night back. He suggested a steak house. I tried to steer him towards seafood or pasta only because I still don't eat meat on Fridays. I know even priests do, but it's just something I've always done. We ended up at a cute Italian Restaurant in New Rochelle. It had been twelve years since I had been on a date. I wasn't sure what to wear, how to act, what to say. I really liked Ted, I kept Faith's words of warning filed near the front of my brain, but I tried to form my own opinions of him and not let something like a feeling or intuition stand in the way of my happiness. There was a part of me that wanted to hold on to the fantasy of a life with Chris, but another part of me knew I needed to move on, and keep him as my best friend.

As the months went on Ted and I grew closer. I even let him meet the kids, something I swore I wouldn't do until I was convinced I had found someone who would be in my life forever. Ted always talked in terms of forever with us. The kids were not thrilled with Ted. They were polite, but after he would leave, they might pass a comment, or I might catch them whispering something to each other. I felt that in time he might grow on them. I wouldn't push it, but I wanted them to all get along. It was becoming evident that we were going to get married.

Faith would call me every few days to say she was thinking of me and praying for me, and she would subtly try to find out if I was still seeing Ted and if everything was okay. I think it eased her mind to find out I was okay, but she always ended the conversation the same way… "Don't lose yourself in him."

I sometimes felt that when I was with him, I was losing myself, but not in the bad way Faith meant. When I kissed him, it was like I was in a whole other world. I think when you kiss someone you should feel lost, like you don't know where you are. You shouldn't have a sense of the here and now when kissing. You should be transported to another place and time, and not be anchored to where you are. I felt like that when I kissed Ted. It was as if there was a melding of our hearts and souls and I always felt dizzy after we stopped kissing.

We were growing closer and closer and it was just a matter of time before I knew he would ask me to marry him. He already talked about moving down to Eastchester to cut down on the travel. He was going to take his girls out of their school and move down here with them. He knew I wouldn't live with him without being married. We talked about buying a house big enough for the six of us. He was fun to be with and made me feel special when we were together.

We were meeting one night after work and he said he had talked to his ex-wife Sharon and had something important to talk to me about. This was it. I knew he wanted to present her with the divorce papers, and he wanted to tell me that she signed and now we were free to get married. I was so excited all day in anticipation of seeing him.

"Hi Ted" I gave him a huge hug and didn't give him a chance to return my greeting. Usually we just melted into each other's arms. Instead I felt a coldness. It was like what I experienced from Billy when I told him I was pregnant with Olivia. "What's wrong?"

"…Nothing…really…we have to talk" I didn't like his tone. He sounded so serious, not his usual goofy lightheartedness. It was frightening. Maybe there was something wrong with the girls or with him. I didn't know what was going to come out of his mouth next. "I spoke to Sharon today."

"Right. So, what happened?" I was afraid to ask.

"Well, we talked about a lot of things and she reminded me of things I had forgotten, and when I presented her with the divorce papers she started to cry and I realized I still had feelings for her."

"Feelings?" I said with the heaviest sarcasm in my voice.

"Yes." I was and wasn't prepared for the next sentence. "We are going to give it another try." I could not speak. I felt as if I had just been punched hard in the stomach. "I'm sorry, but this is good-bye. I have to go back to her. Look, I guess what I felt for you really wasn't love, and I never really saw you as a long-term possibility anyway."

He just left me standing there. I could not move, couldn't cry, couldn't speak, and couldn't think. What did he just say? Where was I? Had I dreamt all this? What on earth was going on? After standing there for what seemed to be an hour, I just got into my car and mechanically tried to drive back home. I couldn't. I needed to figure out what had just happened. I called Faith and the tears could not be controlled. She offered to meet me in Stamford, which was about our halfway point. We went to a diner and I just cried for the rest of the night.

She tried to comfort me, and she was good at it. Not once did she say "I told you so" even though she had every right to. She just said there was something innately evil about him and I was so lucky he was out of my life. He would have only dragged me down. She said I needed to concentrate now on my kids. She asked me how my book was coming along, and I confessed that since I returned from Concord with Ted in my life, I had put it down and had not really done anything with it. She made me get a piece of paper and a pen from the waitress and start to make a list of all the bad things I had gone through and how I could use them in the book. I soon began to see that every negative could be turned into a positive and that I had learned a great deal about life and about myself from each experience, so that each negative was a positive. I needed time that night to grieve losing Ted, but with Faith's help I quickly realized that I had so much going for me, that I would be all right. This was just a black period I was going through.

He was leaving me for his ex-wife, or so he said. I knew there was more to the story than that.

Ted Chapter 33

Well, I did call her when I got back, and we did start dating. It was the most wonderful five months of my life. When I was with Lucy, I felt like I was shedding an old layer of skin just like a snake does. I told her I loved her. We planned on a future. She loved my girls and they loved her. That was really key for me. I couldn't have anyone in my life that didn't get along with my girls. It was bad enough they didn't care much for their own mother; I couldn't bring another woman into the picture that they didn't get along with. I admit I didn't make much of an effort to get close to her kids. They were nice and all, I just didn't really care if they liked me or not.

I even finally got the nerve up to go to a lawyer and have new papers drawn up to finally divorce Sharon and close that Chapter of my life. I could tell Lucy was very old-fashioned and wouldn't sleep with me right away. After I promised her this was a forever thing, and I was going to divorce Sharon, she loosened up a bit and finally after a few months we slept together. It was the most amazing experience of my life. I felt positively transformed. I could feel a change in me. It was like I was being bathed in light and goodness. I hadn't felt this free since the day-before-the-day I met Sharon.

I felt a tremendous turmoil, though starting within me. For some reason, I couldn't stop thinking of Sharon. I didn't want to think of her, I only wanted to think of Lucy, but she was invading my thoughts like a very unwelcome guest. I figured the only way to rid myself of Sharon was to present her with the divorce papers and finally be done with it. I was really scared to do this. I hate confrontation. I knew she wouldn't like this at all, but if it was the only way I could be with Lucy I had to do it. I had to keep feeling the way Lucy made me feel.

I called Sharon and said I needed to talk to her. I asked her to come out for a cup of coffee. I presented her with the papers and told her it was time we end this. At that moment I got a strange feeling in my chest, just like the one I had the day I asked her out for the first time, only this time instead of it giving me strength, it seemed to be debilitating me. I felt like I was being reminded of something that I had promised to do long ago, and it didn't matter what I wanted, I couldn't get out of this commitment. It was a look on her face that said, 'you can't get out of my grips so don't even bother.' I felt as though I was fighting a battle I could only win by giving up my life. There was a feeling of sheer powerlessness and hopelessness that devoured me. I tore up the papers and mechanically took Sharon home.

I saw Lucy and told her that I couldn't go through with the divorce. Sharon and I were going to give it another shot then I quickly left. I felt like such a coward, and I knew I was, I just couldn't stop the words coming out of my mouth. It was as if they were planted there by some other power. It wasn't me speaking at all. Lucy was the one true, good, decent part of my life besides my girls and I was throwing her away and I didn't even know why.

Lucy Chapter 34

When Ted left me, I went into a deep depression. One like I had never experienced before. I didn't feel like myself at all. Even when Billy was at his worse, I was still able to keep it together for the sake of the kids. This time, I was a wreck. I cried at the drop of a hat, I broke down in front of customers, I stopped working on my book. I was very much out of control. Physically I was going through something also. My period wasn't coming, I felt nauseated all the time. I thought my body was just breaking down because of all this. It had been such a shock and let down to think one minute I had found happily-ever-after and then have it all crumble before me. What made it worse in my eyes was the fact that he denied ever having feelings for me. How could he try to pretend we only had a friendship? We had been so intimate, not just physically, but emotionally. That is what hurt the most. If he had only dealt with me honestly throughout the course of our relationship and said he wasn't in love with me, but he told me every day how much he loved me. If only he could have said that he loved me, but he was doing what he thought was best for his children, I would have understood that and respected him for that, but to deny he ever had feelings for me, and tell me he didn't think of me as a "long-term possibility" really and truly devastated me.

So, I cut him out of my life.... until he sent me an e-mail. It was a cold, impersonal business-related email. He had the nerve to ask if I would donate some chocolate to a fundraiser for one of his girl's classes. I could not believe the utter audacity of this man to actually ask a favor and not have the decency to say anything about our breakup. Not an apology, not even a 'Wow, I exercised really poor judgment, nothing. I was going to ignore it, but my blood was boiling over at this point, and my hormones were jumping around out of control. I just had to lash out. I sent him back a scathing email telling him exactly what I thought of him. I held back no punches. After I clicked the "send" button, I felt better. He sent me back one equally as nasty. His reaction infuriated me.

I point blank asked him in one of the e-mails why he couldn't just apologize to me. He finally gave me an answer that stunned me.

"To be perfectly honest, I am not sorry for having met you. We had five wonderful months together. I am sorry for the way it ended and that you are hurting now. I must tell you that you were right on the money about my relationship with Sharon. There is no love there. I haven't felt love since the last time I held you in my arms, and I know I will never feel love like that again. I have been miserable since we broke up, but I chose this path and now I must live with it."

Did I feel sorry for him? Was this the response I was looking for? Was it enough of an apology? Was he fishing for me to take him back? My head was spinning, and I just didn't know what to think of this. In the meantime, I knew something was wrong with me. I was never late, and I was feeling rather tired also. I decided to go to the doctor. I was attributing my lateness to the fact that I had been under so much stress. Instead, the doctor confirmed that I was two months pregnant.

I could not believe the words coming out of the doctor's mouth. I thought for sure he was mistaken. We had been very careful, but I know nothing is foolproof. All the emotions that flooded in my head when I got this news about Olivia and Joey came back to me. I was envisioning my mother's response to this latest news. This would be the third and final installment in the 'Lucy only knows how to screw up' trilogy that I had written in her eyes. I had just gotten back into my mother's good graces and now I would be on the outs again. I was, of course, as always delighted by the news, but not at all delighted by the choice of fathers in this scenario. Even though Billy was so mean to me, he did have a heart. Ted was ruthless in his selfishness and I really didn't want him anywhere near this baby. If there was a way to keep him away, I would. Even though he had just confessed that he loved me, and he missed me, I was not going to forget how he hurt me. Every time I let my guard down with Billy and tried to forgive him and forget what he did, he danced back into my life and hurt me again. Enough was enough. What a mess.

What would my kids think? What kind of role model was I to my teenagers if I was pregnant and unmarried? I was everything I told them not to be. I had to pray a lot over this. I called Father Joe.

"Hi Father, It's Lucy."

"Lucy! How are you, my child? What a nice surprise. How are the children? How are you?"

The kids are great father, how are you."

"I'm wonderful, Lucy, but you didn't tell me how you are. What's wrong?"

The tears started welling up and I couldn't stop them from choking me, so much that I could barely speak. "I did it again Father..."

"Lucy, the last time you said that you were pregnant with Joey...are you...?"

"Yes, Father."

"Is it that wonderful man Ted you told me all about? You two were so much in love! Is this not wonderful news?"

I tried to regain control over my voice so I could finish my conversation with him. "He left me Father, to go back to his wife."

"You mean his ex-wife?"

"No Father, he never was divorced. I deluded myself into thinking that an eight-year separation was just as good as a divorce, but I guess he never went through with the divorce because he still had feelings for her. I feel like such a fool!"

"Lucy, you are one of the smartest women I know, but you have always had one problem. You have a heart that is way too big. You lead with that heart and it always gets you hurt. So, does he know about the baby yet? How far along are you?"

"He doesn't know yet. I'm just about eight weeks pregnant. I was so sick over losing him, and had stopped eating and sleeping, I never would have guessed I was pregnant, not just depressed."

"Is there any chance of you reconciling?"

"He says he still loves me, but he'll stay with her for the sake of his children."

"But this is his child too."

"I'm sure he won't be as connected to this child as his original two."

"I am so sorry you are going through this, Lucy. You have truly been dealt a difficult hand, but God has a plan for you. You are one of his favorites. I tell you that all the time. Look at how things worked out with your other two pregnancies? You have beautiful remarkable teenagers that are simply exemplary human beings. You have done a marvelous job with them, and you will do a marvelous job with this baby as well. I have no doubt that you will come through this stronger, and more blessed by God's love. I think you should tell him and call me after you do to tell me his reaction."

"Thanks, Father, I will."

"God bless you, my child."

I fired up my computer and sent an e-mail telling him the results of my doctor's visit. I couldn't call him for fear that she might be there, and I didn't want to open up a whole can of worms with her. So, I chose to use his preferred, cowardly method of communication. I felt it was a cold way of delivering such news, but I was sure that once he got the news, he would call me.

I waited and waited and got no reply. I knew he read it. I could check the status of it, and it said it was read at exactly 9:01 pm. It was now 11:30 pm and I could barely keep my eyes open and I was tired of checking for new mail, so I flipped off my bedroom light and went to sleep. I was up an hour later at 12:30 am. I checked the computer again. Still no response. I tried to go back to sleep, but at 2:03 am I was checking my e-mail again. I checked it again at 3:46 am, 4:19 am, and 5:35 am. My alarm went off at 6:00 am. I had probably just finally fallen asleep fifteen minutes prior to the ringing. I felt awful. How had he slept knowing I was carrying his child? I could barely deal with it all.

The downside to running your own business is that you can't call in sick. Fortunately, I didn't have any orders to get out that day, but I did have a large wedding order for the weekend. I would get it done. Olivia was such a help. Joey too. They were great workers and I paid them just like I paid all my other workers, but they always put out their best efforts and never acted as though they were more important than anyone else who worked there. They knew it would have been disrespectful to the other workers if they didn't put forth a 100% effort, and it would be uncomfortable if I showed favoritism. I really had raised great kids, and in spite of their father, this next baby would be great too.

I finally decided to say "Uncle" to the alarm clock and get out of bed. As I stepped onto the floor, I was doubled over in pain and felt a sudden warm wet rush between my legs. I sat back on the edge of the bed. I didn't want to believe it but seeing the blood pool I was now sitting in gave me no choice but to believe it. I grabbed my robe and stuffed it between my legs to try to stop the flow of blood long enough for me to get out of bed. I couldn't move. The room was spinning, and I just had to lie back down for fear I would fall off the bed. Olivia poked her head in my room.

"Mom, you're sleeping in?"

"Yes, sweetie, I didn't sleep too well last night."

"You feeling ok?"

"I'm fine, just tired."

"Ok, I have early band rehearsal…see ya…Joey's already at football practice, I'll lock the door."

"Ok, love you!" I was trying to keep my voice steady in spite of the incredible pain I was in.

"Love you too, Mom" I needed her help, but I couldn't tell her what was happening. When I heard the lock clink shut, I just lay in bed staring at the ceiling. I was having enormous cramps and could feel the gush of blood lessoning. I didn't want to risk fainting, so I stayed in bed for another hour. I called Mary and asked her if she wouldn't mind coming in a little earlier to open today. She said no problem. I called my doctor and told him what was happening. He wanted to see me right away. I told him I couldn't get down there. He said he would send an ambulance to come get me. I begged him not to. I didn't want it getting back to the kids that there had been an ambulance at the house. Then he said the most amazing thing!

"I'm coming over." I didn't think I heard him correctly, then he added "Lucy, when my little girl was in the hospital last year with a broken leg you were there almost every day with some little chocolate treat and a smile. I never forgot your kindness. Let me do this for you."

"Thank you, Brian." I really was blessed. Where do you find doctors today that make house calls? "There's a key under the third white rock outside. Just let yourself in…" I thought about calling Chris, but I was too embarrassed to tell him another man in my life had hurt me. I just wanted to hear his comforting southern drawl and feel as though all would be right with the world once again. My next phone call was to Rico. I really needed his support right now. I knew he was too far away to do anything, but his voice was soothing and gave me comfort.

Brian looked me over and confirmed I had a miscarriage. He said because I wasn't too far along, I would recover rather quickly, but not to try to push myself. I should take it easy for a couple of days. He brought me some medication to help my uterus contract but warned me I needed to stay in bed because it would make my legs feel week and crampy. I needed to get the laundry done before the kids got home, so I very slowly and carefully got myself showered, dressed, and put fresh sheets on the bed. I had called Mary to say I thought I had a touch of the flu and would be staying upstairs today. She brought me up lunch and was so kind to me. Other than the leg pain I was starting to feel a bit better physically, but I felt so empty inside. The enormity of what had happened started to hit me. I just lost a child. So did Ted, and he didn't even acknowledge it.

I toyed with the idea of checking to see if he had responded to my e-mail, but I just felt too weak. At this point, he was very low on my list of concerns. I expected the phone to ring any moment now and have it be him telling me he saw my e-mail and was thrilled with the idea of having another child. Then I would have to break the news to him that I had lost the baby. Maybe it would bring us closer, maybe it would drive and irremovable wedge between us. Either way there would be finality. I needed closure.

I slept most of the day no doubt catching up on all the lost sleep from the night before. I was startled awake by the ring of the telephone around 3:15pm. I almost knocked it to the ground in answering it. I knew it wasn't the kids because both had practices until five o'clock, so maybe it was Ted.

"Hello, hello?" There was a momentary silence.

"Good afternoon Ma'am, can I speak to the person in charge of the long-distance service in the house?"

"I'm sorry. I'm not interested." Click. I am usually so nice to solicitors, but I just couldn't deal with one today. A few seconds later the phone rang again. I was very weak and decided to let the machine pick up. If it was Ted, I could grab the phone. I thought I heard Chris's voice on the other end, but I so out of it at that point that I thought I must be dreaming. He was on tour. Well, now that I was up, I decided to pull my laptop over and try to check my e-mail. It seemed like an endless wait for the connection to the Internet to go through. Once it did, I heard the familiar "You've Got Mail!"

I anxiously opened my inbox to find this reply from Ted.Harmon; "Well then, presuming the baby is mine, I guess we will have to figure out a way to deal with this."

That's it? That's the reply I lost sleep over? That was what I got in lieu of a phone call? My God, this man was a cold heartless bastard. How did I ever love him? I fired back a reply

"Well, I guess you won't have to deal with anything. I woke up in a pool of blood this morning. I lost the baby. You may not understand this, but I feel very empty inside. I lost something very precious today, and so did you."

As soon as I hit the send button, I blocked all incoming e-mail from him. If he wanted to see how I was feeling or apologize for his abominable behavior, he would have to call me and hear my voice. I never heard from Ted Harmon again. Good riddance.

I called Father Joe and told him all that happened. He said that the hurt and pain I had suffered from this man, as excruciating as it was, would have been so much worse if this relationship had continued. He said I can always trust Jesus and to only put my trust in Him, and He would take care of me. He said this man was the devil and I was fortunate he left my life, and I did not get sucked into his trap. God protected me and watched over me.

Father Joe always knew just what to say to make me feel better. I knew I could go on and heal and recover from this. It was time for me to take my next dose of medicine. After I took the pill I had to lie down again. I felt sicker than I had felt all day. Something was very wrong I vaguely recall looking at the clock and seeing that it was 4:30 pm. The kids would be home soon. I would have to tell them I was sick and had to go to the hospital. I did not want to do this, but I was really scared. I never felt this bad before.

Olivia came in at 5:00 pm and Rico walked in right behind her. She was delighted and a bit surprised to see her Uncle but did not think it meant anything since he was very unpredictable and popped by often, especially around dinner time. I could not believe what a Godsend he was. I could have him take me to the hospital and the kids would not have to be put through this. I would have to tell him what happened, but he was such a good brother, I was sure he would understand.

I can remember telling Rico what was happening and asking him to wait outside while I dressed. I am not too sure what happened after I dressed. It was all fuzzy. I do remember feeling his presence next to me the whole time I was in the emergency room. It was a very peaceful feeling that flooded over me when I was with Rico. I just felt so comfortable when I was with him. It was like I was home. Rico was a good man. He was kind and honest and patient. I felt goodness coming from him, so unlike the way I felt with Ted which was that somehow something was being sucked out of me when I was near him. My brother saved my life tonight.

Rico stayed by my side until I finally felt better. "You'll have to excuse me, there's someone who needs the shit beat out of him." Normally I would try to stop Rico from his biker justice, but I was too tired to try to stop him, and probably felt that Ted deserved it.

Ted Chapter 35

I had to make some kind of contact with Lucy, and I couldn't call her because I knew if I heard that soft, sexy voice of hers I would melt and then I couldn't go through with this, so I sent her an e-mail under the pretense that I needed her to donate some chocolate to one of my girl's schools. I waited for a response and the response I got floored me. She wrote back saying how hurt she was by all that had transpired and that she was pregnant. I wanted to leap for joy. A child with Lucy, what could be better? I could definitely leave Sharon now. This would give me the courage to do it.

I immediately picked up the phone and called Sharon and told her I was getting new papers drawn up and I was leaving her because Lucy was pregnant. She immediately planted the seed of doubt in my head that maybe it wasn't my baby, and I would be a fool to throw away my old family and start a new one with this woman. She dictated a very cold email that I should send Lucy and I obeyed almost robotically. It hurt me to do this to Lucy, but Sharon gave me no other options. My next e-mail from Lucy was telling me she miscarried our baby. I was devastated. There is nothing more important to me than my girls and the thought of having another little one with Lucy was the only ray of hope I had in this death sentence of a life I was living. Now that hope was gone. I was sitting alone on my pumpkin, but I didn't like it. I wanted Lucy, I wanted that baby, I didn't want to be with Sharon, but she had me in her grips and I couldn't get out of it. I clearly remembered the day at work when I said I would sell my soul to the devil if only I could have Sharon. You must be very careful what you ask for.

Chris Chapter 36

I left David Henry's with a new sense of purpose. Back in my room I reflected on all the events of this past week. I was definitely going to record this new album and make no apologies for it. I had written four songs while I was here. They were so much more like what I used to write back when I had heart and soul in it. I was proud of these songs. I haven't been able to say that for the last 10 years. All I could think about was sharing this news with Lucy.

I pulled out my cell phone to call her. It was such a knee jerk reaction. Every time I had good news, I called Lucy. Every time I had bad news, I called Lucy. Every time I had any high or low or in between I called Lucy. I started to think about David and his Mary and how he let her slip through his fingers and now 50 years later he still regrets doing it. Did I want that to be me at age sixty-seven? I didn't want to spend all this money on just me. I wanted to enjoy it and enjoy it with Lucy. We could have kids. She's such a great mom...She's the woman I want raising my children. We'd have to get a move on it, her clock's a tickin' away, but we could do it.

I finally have a plan. I know what I am going to do. I'll take these next 2 months to start winding down my schedule, while I work on my acoustic album. Then, I am all hers. Lucy has been asked to display her chocolates in the lobby of the World Trade Center in September. I'll be in the city doing a concert at the Garden the night before, so I will surprise her and stop by. I am going to ask her to marry me. No more wastin' time. This is it.

Billy Chapter 37

The summer is almost over, and it is a beautiful September day. I don't know how I am going to show Lucy the new me, but I know I have to make my move soon. The kids said that cowboy singer's been calling a lot and that mom seems to really like him. He's filthy rich, younger than me, talented. I am no match for him. I just can't believe he loves Lucy more than I do. No one can. My life revolves around making her happy. There's nothing I wouldn't do for her. I rubbed the keychain for a little encouragement. I have to show her how much I care about her. I decided I would ask her to lunch and hope and pray that she will accept. I need to tell her how I feel about her. The kids said she was setting up a chocolate display in the World Trade Center on Tuesday. I'll ask her to meet me for lunch. I work right down the street from the towers. I know she doesn't get to the city often; this will be a perfect opportunity.

Rico Chapter 38

I am so lucky to have Diana in my life. She's doing so much better than she was when I first met her. We got married last spring and we're expecting our first baby this September. I hope I can do as good a job as Lucy has done with Olivia and Joey. In spite of their wacko father, they really shine. I may not be the perfect dad, but I'll never hurt my kids, or their mother and they will have more love than they'll know what to do with! Diana will be a great mom. She's got a heart of gold. I can't wait 'til the due date, on September 11th.

Lucy Chapter 39

I could not believe I was setting up my chocolate display in the lobby of the World Trade Center. Thousands of people would see my work. This was such an honor I couldn't imagine why of all the chocolatiers in New York, I was chosen for this. I got there early, 5am to be exact. I drove in and unloaded my car carefully. It' s a little bit hard maneuvering around the city, and it was one of those times when I wished I had a husband to help me, but then I think of how far I have come on my own, and it makes me proud.

Around 8:00 am people were buzzing all-around my display. Many took my cards, and many stopped to ask me about certain pieces. This was meant as a showcase of artistic chocolate design, but I seemed to be drumming up new customers which was an added surprise. I don't get into the city that much, so I am always a bit shocked to see how everyone moves so mechanically. They seem to walk as if rehearsed in perfect rows following the rules of traffic, even when indoors. I often thought about how exciting it must be to work in the city but exhausting as well. I guess Chris and his down-home sensibilities are wearing off on me. I wondered if he would ever ask me to marry him. I wondered if I really ever could be married to him. I would have to leave the chocolate shop and follow him on the road or get used to being without him for long stretches of time. I wasn't sure if the kids could adapt to either lifestyle. I've also been thinking a great deal about Billy. I don't have feelings for Billy in a romantic way, but he was my first love and gave me the greatest two gifts in my life, so I was hoping he could get his life together and eventually find happiness. The kids have been telling me how much he's changed. They say he's much calmer. He's called a few times, and I can sense a difference in his voice. He is a more relaxed, even person. He finally took my advice and went to a doctor to find out what was wrong with him. As I suspected, there really was something medically wrong with him. I knew deep down he loved me, and that it was not really him who was blowing up at me all the time, but a demon he couldn't control.

There are times when I think I was a horrible person for leaving him. I should have insisted he get help instead of just walking away from him. If he had lost a leg or an arm, or had an incurable illness, I would have stayed with him, his illness is of his mind. He has bipolar disorder, and it is just as crippling as if he was an amputee. How could I walk away from him? Then there was another part of me that just could not go back to the life of uncertainty I had with Billy. I lived my life walking on eggshells when I was with him. I couldn't trust him, no matter how much I may have once loved him.

Just before 9:00 am I heard a lot of sirens go off and someone said a plane hit the tower. I felt so bad. I thought some poor solo pilot got lost and mistakenly flew into the building. I hoped he had survived and continued passing out my brochures. A few moments later I noticed many firemen in the building. I didn't smell smoke, so I figured they were just here to do a drill. Then people started swarming out of the tower. I tried to ask what was happening, but no one would speak, they just were running. The sirens were deafening, there were people all over the place and I didn't know what to do. Someone finally told me that a second plane hit this tower, and everyone needed to evacuate immediately. I grabbed my purse which I had stashed under the table and at that moment I felt something burning in the back of my neck. The table collapsed on top of me and I was trapped. I tried to scream for help, but no one heard me. I heard someone say the first tower was falling. My mind could not even get around what that meant. How could something so massive fall? Was this all a dream? I did not remember much after that, I blacked out.

Billy Chapter 40

My paralegal ran into my office crying and told me what happened. I turned on the radio and could not believe what I was hearing. The first tower fell and the second was going. I knew Lucy was in tower two. I had to get there. I had to find her. I called her cell phone, but there was no service. I ran out of my building and sprinted to the towers. Everybody was heading out of the towers, but I was heading in. I was stopped by a few people who told me I had to turn around, but I had to find Lucy. I was to meet her later that day for lunch to talk about how I'd changed and tell her I wanted her to take me back. I had to have the chance to tell her I had changed and that I did it all for her. I had to find her. I was choking from the thick dust in the lobby. I was like a salmon swimming upstream while the sea of people were fleeing in the opposite direction. I could smell only smoke and dirt, but then I got the very slightest whiff of the most wonderful smell in the world, chocolate. I saw Lucy's sign, "Chocolations" and knew this was where I would find her. I called for her, but it was too loud to hear anything. I saw her lying under the table bleeding, and unconscious. I tried to reach her, to save her but…

Chris Chapter 41

I heard the sirens, and I knew I needed to find Lucy. There was a heavy cloud of dust everywhere choking me, but I had to find her. Finally, I saw the remnants of her display and saw her small little body crouched under a table. I didn't know if she were alive or dead. I lifted her gently over my shoulder and got her outside and ran as far away from the building as I could. I could feel her breathing which made me run even faster. Just when we got about a block away, the second tower fell. I was relieved to have found her, but the horror of what was happening around me hit me hard. The whole area was a cloud of dust. There were people running and crying everywhere. I set Lucy down gently on the ground and had to stand over her so she wouldn't be trampled. People were all over the place. I took off my shirt and wiped the blood from her head. I was relieved to see that it was just a small cut. Someone handed me a bottle of water which I used to wipe her dirty face. She finally came to. I was so relieved to see her beautiful eyes staring up at me. She asked what happened, but I told her not to try to talk now. Truth is, I didn't know what happened. She was able to get on her feet and putting my arm around her I gently led her uptown.

As soon as we could find a working phone, I called the kids who were frantic having heard the news, knowing their mom was in the towers. Their relief at knowing she was safe was palpable. I was so glad I could do this for her, and for them, and for me.

Lucy Chapter 42

As the days wore on after September 11th, I started to realize exactly what happened. So many lives were lost. So many were still missing and presumed dead. So many heroes emerged from the rubble. Billy was blocks away and ran into the burning building to find me, but his body hasn't been found yet. The kids are inconsolable and I'm in a state of shock myself trying to wrap my head around this whole thing.

Chris saved my life. He carried me over his shoulder for blocks to safety. It became clear to me what kind of man Chris was and what kind of man Billy was. Chris never left my side. In a way, neither did Billy. I feel a tremendous sense of guilt that he died trying to save me. I spent so many years hating the monster he became when he had one of his episodes, that I forgot the good person that lived inside him also. He died trying to make up for all the things he did wrong. A part of me will always love him, and I hope he knows that and found peace.

Rico joined the relief effort even though Diana had just given birth. She knew this was where he had to be. That was the kind of man Rico was. Rico embraced Chris like a brother in gratitude for finding me.

Rico Chapter 43

The best and the worst day rolled up in one. September 11, 2001. Diana gave me a beautiful little baby girl who we named Hope, and the world changed forever. I almost lost my sister, I gained a new 'brother', and my niece and nephew lost their innocence, and their father. I joined the search on the mound because I needed to find Billy's remains and give Olivia and Joey some closure to what happened. I think Lucy needed it too. She loves Chris, but a part of her will always love Billy which is why I didn't kill him when I had the chance.

It changed me. Becoming a father did too. Having a wife and kid made me want to settle into something stable, and I felt the need to help people. I took the test for the fire department and started training for a new career. I'll always march to my own drum, but this is where the beats are now leading me.

Lucy Chapter 44

Chris stayed with me in Eastchester and nursed me back to health and made sure the kids were ok. He seemed in no rush to leave and get back on the road. It was hard for me to understand how there could be so much hatred in the world. I still have flashbacks to that awful day and wake up most nights unable to fall back to sleep because I don't want to relive it in my nightmares. Sometimes my nightmares turned into visions of Billy trying to get to me in the dust, and then he vanishes. The kids are struggling with this too. We have been relying on our faith to get us through this, and Father Joe has been a great comfort.

I also saw the best come out in people. There was a new sense of appreciation in people for every day we are given, and it seemed to serve as a reminder that tomorrow is not a guarantee. Maybe that was why Chris was still here, I didn't question it. I just enjoyed it.

It was late October, and we were out in my backyard on a rare warm autumn evening. I was sitting close to him remembering the day in Lubbock when our 10 plus year friendship started. Every moment with him for the past 10 years was wonderful, but tainted by the reality of who he was, and how our lives would never intersect permanently. This night felt different. This whole month felt different. I finally felt like we were settling into each other and neither of us were going to run away.

"If I haven't told you yet today, thank you for saving my life" I said as I mindlessly traced my fingers through his hair.

"You save my life every day, Darlin, I was just returning the favor" His drawl still melted me. I never felt like I was with a mega star, he was just my best friend, my hero, my love. He might belong to the world, but tonight, he belonged to me.

There was something different about him since 9/11. I had forgotten that he had been in Concord that summer and seemed to be trying to tell me for 2 months what happened on his trip.

"Darlin, remember when I went up to Concord in July and I told you I had an epiphany of sorts? I finally got my head in the right place. I came back and recorded a new album. It's the first one in a long time I am really proud of." He was a little fidgety which always signaled to me that he was about to drop some important news. Usually, it meant he was about to tell me about some major tour, or something that would take him away from me for a very long time. This was a different fidget. "I made a plan in Concord and sketched out how I wanted the next part of my life to go. First, I would make this new album, so I could go out on a high note. I didn't want to leave this business with my last work being the crap I'd been putting out. Second, I cleared my calendar. That's why you've had to deal with my big ugly mug hangin' around you so much."

I had to laugh. It has been like a dream having Chris with me so much. I knew his calendar changed when the world changed on September 11, but I didn't realize until that moment that some of it was by his own doing. Then I realized what he just said. "Chris, am I hearing you right? You're coming off the road?"

"No, Darlin, I am starting on a new road…" With that he got down on one knee and pulled a sparkling diamond ring out of his pocket and slipped it on my finger. "I want you on this new road with me. Please be my wife, and I promise I will never make you second to my music again."

"Yes, yes and YES! Of course I will marry you! Chris, I love you so much!" I almost felt guilty feeling so elated when the rest of the world was still in mourning. But this was a dream come true. Not only did I have Chris, but I had all of him. He was going to focus on us, and we were finally going to build a life together.

Although the scars of 9/11 may never heal, I felt so blessed!

Once I was feeling more like myself, I threw myself back into my work and planning my tomorrows with Chris. The holidays were coming up and the orders were pouring in. I had expanded the shop tremendously from the original tiny storefront I had when Billy and I first came up from New Jersey 13 years ago. I had great workers who I could trust to run things if I needed a day off, so my load was lightened a bit. I had made so many wonderful friends in Eastchester, I had these fantastic kids, and I had finally found a true partner and love in Chris. The tables had turned and now I was the busy one. The difference was Chris was here. He would even put on an apron and help me in the shop from time to time. With Chris's help and star power, I was redefining the business into a more philanthropic endeavor. We worked hard at giving back to the community. We both got to do what we loved and help others with it. I really had a full life.

I still felt as though I had some unfinished business, my book. I wanted it to help some woman perhaps that was battered or in a bad relationship to see that you can rise above the turmoil you are experiencing and redefine tragedy as a positive life. Maybe this is what Father Joe meant when he said, "You are going to inspire multitudes of people someday with your great hope, and optimism, and sheer goodness. This will all pass one day, but the mark you leave on this earth will remain. It will remain through your children, and through the goods works you do."

Olivia Chapter 45

I have to admit, I enjoy staying home with my kids. Mom was home with me and Joey, but I went into law like my dad and had to go back to work right after Lara was born, and then had to return right after I had Eric. This quarantine has become a very precious time for me, Ross and the kids. As much as I hate the disruption to normal life and hate not being able to see Mom and Chris and the twins, Uncle Rico and Aunt Diana, all my cousins, and Joey and Liz, my kids love having their mom and dad home all day, eating dinner together as a family every night, and all the fun new traditions we are coming up with. I've even been channeling my mom and making chocolate with them. It was amazing growing up with a mom like her. Nothing was easy for her, but she made everything look effortless.

I have been doing so much online ordering since the quarantine began. I wasn't surprised to see my UPS driver but was surprised to see the return address on one of the packages he left on my doorstep. NYPD One Police Plaza. A few years ago I submitted a sample of my dad's DNA to an organization that was trying to match people lost in 9/11 with items recovered at the site. In the box was a yellowed cellophane bag with some black sharpie letters scribbled on it. Inside, wrapped in faded tissue, was a laminated key chain.

"In the long run, men hit only what they aim at. Therefore, though should fail immediately, they better aim high." Henry David Thoreau.

ABOUT THE AUTHOR

Maria Valente was born, bred and educated all within a 10-mile radius in Westchester County, NY. She grew up the youngest of five girls in a home built by her father in 1950 which is still in the family today. As a teen she was diagnosed with scoliosis, since corrected by two long, painful surgeries followed by months of physical therapy. This experience led to an appreciation of the struggles of people with physical disabilities. Her creativity and skill as a writer were always praised, but she struggled in school despite her best efforts. A receptive learning disorder was not diagnosed until she was in her late 20's. This was a relief, and explained why she had struggled so much as a young person in school, and spurred her on to accomplish more. She applied and was accepted to law school and studied environmental law. Law was not her love, she graduated, but never practiced. Her many jobs in fields such as real estate, office management and computer training were still not her real love. Her dream was to one day open her own chocolate shop, and to finally write a book. Many more setbacks and hardships tried to defeat her, but she kept on the course. She began this book in 1999 and the bulk of it was written at that time. It took a pandemic to finally get it published in 2020. She has owned her successful Chocolate Shop, *Chocolations*, in Mamaroneck, NY for over 14 years, and this, is her first novel.